THE BUZZARDS
MUST ALSO BE FED

Also by Anne Wingate

DEATH BY DECEPTION
THE EYE OF ANNA

THE BUZZARDS MUST ALSO BE FED

Anne Wingate

Walker and Company
New York

First published in the United States of America in 1991
by Walker Publishing Company, Inc.
Published simultaneously in Canada by Thomas Allen & Son
Canada, Limited, Markham, Ontario

Library of Congress Cataloging-in-Publication Data
Wingate, Anne.
The buzzards must also be fed / Anne Wingate.
p.   cm.
ISBN 0-8027-5773-1
I. Title.
PS3573.I5316B89   1991
813'.54—dc20   90-39888
CIP

Printed in the United States of America

2 4 6 8 10 9 7 5 3 1

I'll have to dedicate this one to Chief Summerford, Colo-nel (now Chief) Denney, Colonel Manly, Major Turner, Major Posey, Major "Doc" Luther, and everybody else who ever told me to get the book out of my pocket, it didn't go with the uniform. Also to Barbara Brackman, who told the story, about my books and me, that I have attributed on page 14 to Quinn about Hansen.

Special thanks to the Legal Counsel Division of the Federal Bureau of Investigation and to Charles Brown of the Warden's Office, Huntsville State Prison, for provid-ing me information. And extra special thanks to Kevin Smith of the Utah State Crime Laboratory for not only providing information, but also taking the time to look it up.

Prologue

THE ROAD WAS A sheet of ice.

There were no sanding trucks out because there was no sand. In places where it does not freeze, no preparations are made for ice.

About noon on March 17, when it was already late spring and beginning to feel like summer in South Texas, a freak storm swept south from the Panhandle. By the time Steve Hansen left the courtroom at four o'clock after another hearing that might as well never have happened, for all the good it did him, and clambered awkwardly into a prison station wagon, it felt like winter in North Dakota.

He wasn't dressed for winter, in North Dakota or anywhere else. He was wearing denim jeans without a belt, a short-sleeved white T-shirt, a light denim jacket, a long-sleeved blue chambray shirt, and sneakers without laces. No belt, no shoelaces, nothing that anybody considered that by any extreme stretch of imagination he could use to hang himself with. He supposed if he wanted to work at it he could figure out a way to hang himself with the jeans when he took them off, but he didn't see any need to try. He wasn't the one who'd decided he might be suicidal.

He was also wearing an assortment of hardware that included handcuffs, leg irons, and a chain that ran up the front of his body from his ankles to his wrists and was secured to another chain that circled his waist.

Nobody worried that he was being driven back to Huntsville State Prison by only one guard. In the backseat, in the cage, wrapped up in forty pounds of chain and buckled into a seat belt he couldn't reach to unbuckle, even Steve Hansen couldn't cause trouble.

The car was an hour north of Houston, halfway to Huntsville, when it hit the ice. The guard hadn't been listening to weather forecasts. He could see that the sky was pitch dark, and he could hear the rain hitting the roof of the car, but he was used to driving in darkness and rain. That didn't bother him. There was no reason why it should. When the pellets of sleet began to pile up on the windshield, he swore and slowed down a little, but took no other precautions.

He was driving fifty miles an hour when he began to skid. He didn't stay on the road long after that. The station wagon flew across three largely unoccupied lanes of traffic, rolled completely over in the ditch, and came to rest against a pine tree, upright again, with all four doors and the tailgate gaping open.

Steve Hansen, held in place in the middle of the back seat, twisted around to unfasten the seat belt he wasn't supposed to be able to reach. Then he scrambled out of the car, to reach awkwardly into the front seat around the unconscious guard and jerk the keys out of the ignition.

Without haste despite the cold and the cramped position of his arms as he worked, he unlocked all the chains and stood for a moment erect in the sleet, a free man for the first time in three years.

Then he leaned over the guard again, to check first for pulse, for evidence of serious injury, before relieving him of his gunbelt, wallet, and identification. With the identification in his pocket, the gunbelt buckled on, and the pistol a familiar weight on his right hip, he methodically checked the car. There ought to be a blanket...

There was, in the far back. He got it out and tucked it neatly around the guard. *You'll be conscious again, able to reach shelter, before you have time to freeze to death. Stupid mutt,* Hansen thought, closing the doors as well as he could against the wind, *you buckled my seat belt. Why in the hell didn't you think to buckle your own?*

Shivering from the sleet dripping down the back of his neck and the constant wind, slipping on the ice, Steve Hansen walked toward the south. Probably he'd find a ride quickly. He looked like a small-town deputy sheriff, with his short haircut, the denim, and the gunbelt, and he could always think up a good story. If he didn't get a lift, it wouldn't matter. He was moving too fast to freeze. He had just over a hundred miles to go; he could walk that in four days, maybe three. There'd be plenty of water. There wasn't much money in the wallet, but he'd be able to eat a little. If he did get hungry, what difference did that make? He wasn't going to starve in four days.

Steven Hansen was on his way to Bayport, Texas, to kill a man. A man who had no right to stay alive, after the damage he'd done to so many people's lives. A man the law couldn't—or wouldn't—touch.

He had to accomplish that, not for revenge, which he'd

always considered a stupid motive, nor for the sake of those who were already dead. They were safe now; nothing else could harm them. Not even for his own sake, because he was man enough to take whatever came. No, he had to do it for the sake of whatever lives that evil was touching now or might touch next.

After he killed Dale Shipp, he didn't much care what happened to him.

$\triangledown$

Chapter 1

"H'LO, BOSS," AL Quinn said.

Mark Shigata lifted one eyebrow. "Boss?"

Quinn shrugged. "I gotta call you something. We both know I can't say your first name." Shigata nodded; he'd never met Mark Quinn, killed by a hit-and-run driver at fifteen, but he knew the Quinns still grieved as if Mark had been an only child rather than one of twelve. "And calling your friends by their last names gets kinda wearisome. At least it does to me. So—boss."

"I'm not a cow," Shigata said.

"Sorry," Quinn said, grinning. He hadn't realized Shigata, like him, had seen cows milked, had heard the milker's soothing "Soo-boss" as the cow moved restlessly in the stanchion.

"If it suits you—" Shigata left the sentence unfinished. "Your promotion came through."

"Like it means something."

"It means about thirty more bucks a week in your paycheck."

"Which'll go out faster'n it comes in."

"So? At least you've got it to go out. I realize you'd get more in Houston, but—"

"I'd be lucky to make patrolman in Houston, let alone

1

captain," Quinn interrupted. "You've got a wife, why'n't'cha go home to her?"

Instead, Shigata sat down on the edge of a desk. "What's wrong, Al?" he asked quietly.

Quinn wiped his hand across his beefy face. "Is it that obvious?"

"It's that obvious. What's wrong?"

Quinn shook his head. "You don't want to hear it."

"Okay." Shigata stood up. "You change your mind, give me a shout."

"I'm sorry," Quinn said a little shamefacedly. "It's just— this one I've gotta work out for myself."

"Okay. If anything comes up, let me know. Otherwise, I'll be back about five A.M. And damn twelve-hour shifts, anyway."

"How long are we gonna go on like this?"

"Until we manage to hire somebody that's not a rookie. And with the package we've got to offer, I don't think that's likely to happen anytime in the next two or three days."

"Or months, or weeks, or years," Quinn agreed. "Would you have come to work here if you'd known it was going to be like this? Twenty officers counting you, five civilians? Nobody but you and me with more than a year in harness?"

"I'll tell you a story," Shigata said, seating himself again. "One time when I was stationed in Georgia, in a town just a little bit bigger than this one, I was talking to a policewoman. It was pretty obvious just from talking with her that she was well-educated and intelligent, and I started asking questions and found out she had a master's degree. So I asked, 'Can't a woman with your mind and education find anything better to do than be a South Georgia cop?' She kinda looked at me and answered, very softly, 'No. No, I can't.' I thought that over, and then I realized what she meant. Well—I can't find anything better to do than be the police chief of Bayport, Texas. Even with all the problems. We'll manage, Al. If we don't hire somebody with experience eventually, we'll grow our own."

"If they'll stop leaving every time they get some experi-

2

ence," Quinn answered dourly. "Are you going home, or are you gonna stay up here all night?"

"I'm going home. Oh, yeah, you did know they closed the causeway, didn't you?"

"How come?"

"Don't you ever listen to weather reports?"

"When would I have time?"

"We got an ice storm coming in. It went through Huntsville about five, s'posed to be here by six-thirty or so."

Quinn swore, colorfully and comprehensively. "My garden's about all up. Now I'm gonna have to replant everything. All right, all right, why don't you go home? I'll skid around all night—"

"Try not to. We've got two cars in the shop already."

The eighteen-wheeler managed to stop not more than fifty feet past Hansen despite the ice, and Hansen sprinted toward it. He clambered up as the driver opened the door. "Thanks," he said. "It's getting mighty damn cold out there. I'm Rusty Claiborne." *I might have to produce some identification. The identification I've got belongs to Rusty Claiborne. Got to hope like hell he doesn't look close at pictures—and hope Rusty hasn't woke up yet, or at least if he has they haven't got it on the air yet.*

"Hank Murphy here. So what's a smoky doing out on foot in this kinda weather? You are a smoky, ain't you?"

Hansen nodded, rubbing his hands together in the welcome heat of the truck cab. "Yeah," he said, easily imitating the uneducated speech of the real Rusty Claiborne. Too easily. After three years on Death Row, he wasn't sure he'd ever be able to get himself back. If he ever got the chance. Not that he expected to. He doubted he'd live another week. "Tryin' to get way down I-45. Spun out about ten miles back, and I've been walkin' ever since. We can send somebody back to pick up the car later, but I need to get home *now*."

"I hear that. So how far's home?"

"Bayport."

"Hell, when you said way down I-45, you meant it, didn't

you? There ain't much more of I-45 after Bayport."

"Fourteen miles," Hansen agreed. "Fourteen miles from the Bayport exit till you fall off into the Gulf."

Murphy chuckled. "Yeah, if you been poppin' too many reds and ain't got sense enough to stop. I heard about this driver one time, he druv right off the seawall, and when the deputies got down there he was a-settin' out on the hood tryin' to feed bennies to the bulldog. You know, the hood ornament, the bulldog? Damned if he wasn't trying to feed bennies to the bulldog."

"Yeah, they'll get to you sure as shootin', if you ain't got sense enough to stop takin' 'em," Hansen agreed easily. "So how far are you going?"

Murphy looked at him sharply, and Hansen realized, uneasily, that the last sentence had been himself, not Rusty Claiborne. But maybe it didn't matter. Murphy, he figured, had popped a few bennies himself in the last couple of hours. *You're not on duty, Hansen. You'll never be on duty again.*

"Not quite far enough for you," Murphy said after the pause. "I'm pulling off in League City, gonna spend the night there and unload in the A.M. But you oughtn't to have any trouble getting on to Bayport—you smokies do look out for one another."

"Just like you drivers." *Right. That's just what I need. Any cop in Texas'll be real happy to give me a ride—right back to where I came from, if he doesn't just put a bullet through me and claim I tried to run.* "You mind if I catch a little shut-eye?"

"Naw, go ahead, if you don't mind the radio."

Not sleeping. Not sleeping. For three years, every time Hansen closed his eyes he saw it happening all over again. Him and Lillian arguing. They did that maybe once a month but it didn't mean anything, they both knew that, they both were ready to make up the next day. But this had been worse than usual because they were arguing about Gaylene, Gaylene who wasn't his daughter—not really—but he and Lillian had been married when Gaylene was less than a year old and although he'd never formally adopted her they'd entered her in school as Gaylene Hansen, not Gaylene

4

Shipp, without even thinking about it. She'd been Gaylene Hansen ever since.

She was fifteen. A little past fifteen. Wild. Beautiful but wild. Really wild, she made him think of Tamar, Tamar in the Bible and Robinson Jeffers's Tamar and every other Tamar you ever heard of all rolled into one. Long black hair down to her waist and she was built like eighteen, not fifteen. She'd been crying for three days and Lillian knew what was wrong, but Lillian wouldn't tell him and Gaylene wouldn't tell him.

Most likely she was pregnant. A wild girl, fifteen, it wasn't impossible, and if she was that was bad but it wasn't that terrible, nobody was going to throw her out on the street.

But they wouldn't tell him. And he and Lillian fought about it, not about Gaylene but about the silence, and maybe they were fighting not just because of that but also because it was hot and muggy and the moon was full and Todd was in everybody's way making everything worse, not that Hansen could blame him—abscessed tooth and a head full of codeine and penicillin, whining about it being too hot to sleep, which was damn sure true—until Lillian told him to take some more codeine and go sleep on the front porch. Then she went on crying and refusing to explain, until finally Hansen stormed out into the night, away from Gaylene crying in her bedroom, away from Lillian crying in the living room, past Todd asleep on top of his sleeping bag on the front porch. Stormed out away from it all. He'd done that before, not often, but when he was so mad he was afraid he'd hit Lillian if he stayed, then he left. He came back when he cooled off. He always had. He'd told Lillian, one time when they weren't fighting, why he left like that, and she'd said that was okay, she understood.

He'd have come back.

But he drove down to Galveston and stopped at a bar and had a few too many and he wasn't on duty the next day, there wasn't any sense risking driving back when he knew he wasn't fit to drive, so he said the hell with it and drove down to the seawall and got out the sleeping bag they kept

5

in the trunk and went down and slept on the beach.

Which was illegal, but he figured if a Galveston cop—or rather a deputy, the beach is county, not city—came down to check on him, he'd explain why and they'd kinda laugh and tell him not to do it again.

Only one didn't. And it wasn't until the next day he knew he'd regret that the rest of his life.

The next morning, he couldn't get into his own driveway past the police cars and ambulances. So he parked in the street and headed for the house and one of his own subordinates stopped him.

At gunpoint.

From where he was standing he could see the dog; that fat old cocker spaniel. Lillian already had it when he married her. He could tell the way it was lying it was dead, nothing lies quite that way alive. But the old dog must have been seventeen years old, and nobody sends ambulances and cop cars because a cocker spaniel died.

He asked what else was wrong.

And asked, and asked, and finally Chief Shipp came out, his face white and drawn. He gave Hansen a look that would freeze a geyser and said, "You son of a bitch, you know what's wrong."

He didn't know. Not then.

Not until later. Later, when Shipp handcuffed him and led him into his own house to see Lillian lying on the living room floor, a black-rimmed hole in the middle of her forehead, his own service revolver at her feet. To see Gaylene lying facedown on her bed, that long black hair matted with thickening blood. To be told that the boy Todd, his and Lillian's son, had wakened from a drugged sleep on the front porch to find the dead cocker spaniel in the sleeping bag with him, then run indoors and found the other two.

(And why hadn't someone found them sooner? Hansen wondered. Heard the shots, and come to check? But he knew the answer. The neighbors didn't work for the city. They could afford air conditioning. Closed windows, air conditioners humming. They wouldn't hear shots.)

6

"Was it worth it?" Shipp asked harshly. "Was it worth it, whatever you did it for?"

Hansen just stared at him, too numb for speech. They made a lot of that later, during the trial—they showed the videotape the newsmen took, Hansen standing handcuffed on the front porch, his face set, no tears.

Hadn't any of them ever heard of shock?

"You meant it to look like murder-suicide, didn't you?" Shipp said harshly. "Wanted us to think Lillian shot Gaylene and then herself. You damn fool son of a bitch, didn't you remember no woman ever shoots herself in the face?"

Hansen didn't answer. His own pistol lay at Lillian's feet. Yes, he knew women suicides didn't usually put the gun to their faces. But he also knew he hadn't fired the gun. So who else could have fired it except Lillian? What else could it be except murder-suicide?

Then—then—he was even a little sorry for Shipp. Sorry for him because it was easy to see how a man like Shipp would have to have somebody to blame for his daughter's death, even if it was the wrong somebody. Sorry for him, and thinking that once the haze of grief and rage started to lift, maybe then Shipp would listen to reason.

He didn't suspect any reason but scapegoating, for Shipp's insistence that Hansen had to be guilty.

Not then.

Not until two days later, when Shipp's face had lost that look of shock, to take on its familiar aspect of malicious mischief. Not until Hansen started talking alibi and Shipp shrugged and said, "Don't make me no never mind. You might have an alibi, but that boy of yours, he sure don't have one."

That was when Hansen knew.

Knew Shipp knew what had happened that night. Knew it wasn't Steve Hansen, knew it wasn't Todd Hansen, and knew he could pin it on one of them anyway, could keep the attention focussed on the Hansens, so that nobody would ever get to asking around why it was that Dale Shipp's ex-wife and teenage daughter died that way. He didn't care which one of them walked and which one took the rap.

7

But Hansen did care, and Shipp knew Hansen cared.

So Hansen fought the charge with both hands tied behind him. He wanted to walk. But not at his son's expense.

If he could prove it was suicide—if he could prove Lillian shot Gaylene and then herself—then he and Todd both walked. But he couldn't. There were no usable fingerprints on the pistol—at least so Shipp said. Which could mean there were no usable fingerprints, or could mean Shipp had smudged them on purpose.

Firearms residue tests were inconclusive. That didn't mean anything. Firearms residue tests are often inconclusive.

The state brought in psychiatrists to say a woman doesn't shoot herself that way, not in the middle of the forehead. Hansen didn't need psychiatrists for that. He knew a woman doesn't shoot herself that way—usually.

But not usually doesn't mean not ever.

The fact was his wife and stepdaughter had been shot to death with his pistol after he and his wife had quarreled. He couldn't prove he hadn't done it.

He hoped the state couldn't prove he had done it.

But juries are funny. You never can tell about juries.

Shipp and the DA reminded him that when a pet is killed during the course of a family murder you can count on its being a family member did it, because to an outsider the pet is a thing, it's only to the family that the pet becomes family. They brought in a psychiatrist to tell the jury that.

He reminded them it was Lillian's dog, not his. But he didn't say—couldn't say—that the dog had somehow become Todd's dog.

They brought Todd in to testify, over Hansen's protests. Todd wouldn't even look at Hansen as he described the quarrel. When the court-appointed defense attorney asked if they'd quarreled before—after all, most people do—Todd said yes but not like that.

And that was true.

Todd said he didn't know any more than that. He explained about the toothache, the codeine. He said they were still quarreling when he went to sleep.

8

That, too, was true.

They even called in someone to testify about the effects of codeine, to show that Todd really could have slept as soundly as he claimed to.

It was true that Todd was a sound sleeper, even without codeine. He'd slept through quarrels, shouting, crying, banging doors before this.

But gunshots?

Even with codeine?

Hansen wasn't so sure about that. But he had his own suspicions as to why Todd hadn't heard the shots, and he didn't raise them in court because they wouldn't do him any good.

There were a lot of questions Hansen did want to ask that never got asked. There were a lot of things he wanted to say that never got said.

He was convicted all the same. And he'd never been allowed to speak to Todd, even when he was out on bond before the trial, because they kept Todd where he couldn't see him, in case he wanted to kill Todd too.

It wasn't until later, in jail, during the trial, still later on Death Row, that he'd finished putting the pieces together. The whys. The hows.

He was still sure Lillian did it, did kill herself in a way a woman usually doesn't, did kill Gaylene. But why? So Gaylene was pregnant—and he was pretty sure of that—she wasn't by any means the only fifteen-year-old girl ever to turn up pregnant, and these things didn't usually cause murder, or suicide. So the problem—the really bad part— had to be who she was pregnant by.

And no matter how many times Hansen thought it out, it always came back to the same man.

Dale Shipp.

The chief of police.

Lillian's first husband, Gaylene's father.

Gaylene hadn't wanted to see Shipp, never had, and for years Shipp didn't bother, but when she hit thirteen and quit looking like a scrawny little girl then all of a sudden Shipp did want to see her. He said he'd get a court order if he had to. He asked Hansen if he wanted to keep his job.

Well, Hansen didn't. Not that bad. But Lillian did, Lillian was scared. She was scared of what would happen if he didn't have that job, she was scared he couldn't get another, and let's face it, she was scared of Dale Shipp, and Hansen couldn't talk her out of that fear.

So Gaylene visited Shipp every other weekend, because her mother said she had to. And for a while she came home crying every time.

Then she quit crying. About that, about anything. That was when she grew her hair long and turned into Tamar, so that to Hansen it was as if a stranger had taken up residence in the little girl he'd been daddy to. He didn't know her anymore. Nobody knew her anymore.

Now Gaylene was dead. She'd been dead three years, and so had Lillian.

Hansen wanted two things. He wanted five minutes—more if he could get it, but at least five minutes—alone with Todd. Long enough to say, son, I don't care what they told you, I didn't kill your mother, and I didn't kill your sister. I'd never have harmed either of them, and I will never harm you. I'm sorry you've been through this, but it was none of my doing.

That was all. And if Todd was able to listen to that, then there was a lot more he'd say, but just that would be enough if that was all the time he got.

The other thing was, he was going to kill Dale Shipp.

If Todd turned him in then he wouldn't get the chance to kill Shipp, but if he went after Shipp first he definitely wouldn't get the chance to see Todd. There are two things cops hate more than anything else: cop killers, and cops who go bad. After he killed Shipp, they'd think he was both.

Well, to be honest, he would be both. He hadn't killed Lillian or Gaylene, he wasn't a cop gone bad yet no matter what they thought of him, no matter what the courts said, but he was on his way to Bayport to commit premeditated murder.

He didn't want to. Not really, even now. But he couldn't

10

think of any other way to make sure Dale Shipp never demolished another life.

He opened his eyes, to watch the wiper blades chasing sleet across the glass, to listen to a nasal voice complaining about cheating love.

Funny how fast things get to seem normal. It was hard to remember that once he'd had a job he liked in spite of Dale Shipp, a wife and kids he loved despite the occasional quarrels, that he'd once gone home in the evening to eat supper and turn on the TV, like everybody else. A normal ordinary life, and he'd never even thought of the possibility that it could all be gone, literally overnight.

Nobody could go through life thinking that way. There had to be something that seemed normal, even if it was only a stainless-steel toilet in a small barred room, because without the concept of normalcy life has no shape.

A normal night, as normal as things had gotten to be lately. Shigata had insisted on washing the dishes, because Melissa had made dinner and it wasn't fair for her to have to do the dishes too. Melissa looked at him solemnly—she almost never laughed or smiled, even now—and said they'd have to get a dishwasher, it was ridiculous for the chief of police to wash dishes. Gail, at thirteen, wasn't volunteering. She always managed to have a lot of homework about dishwashing time, even if it did mysteriously disappear as soon as the dishes were put away.

That was okay. The Shigatas had been married only seven months; that still counted as newlyweds even if Mark was forty-seven, and kitchens were as good as any other place to kiss a little.

Well, as good as any other place you could reasonably use while a very alert teenager was still awake.

So it was with only half his mind that Shigata noticed the telephone ringing in the living room, until Gail said, "Daddy, it's for you."

It usually was, on that phone. It had become evident six months ago that a separate line for Gail was necessary if

11

Shigata expected any official calls to get through. And Melissa didn't get calls at all, on their line or Gail's. She was still, quietly but firmly, refusing to meet people.

"Shigata." He was holding the dish towel under his arm and Gail was giggling because it draped itself across the butt of the .357 he'd taken to wearing since drug-runners had begun using AK-47s. He supposed sooner or later he'd have to switch over to an automatic, as so many other police were doing, but he'd tried that once, years ago when he was still in the Bureau, and the gun jammed on him at an exceedingly bad time. He wasn't likely to forget that soon. He had a scar to remind him.

He never took the pistol off, even at home, until he took his clothes off, because when Quinn needed him Quinn needed him fast.

"We got problems." Quinn's voice sounded tight.

"What kind of problems?"

"How long ago did you move here from Denver?"

"What difference does that make?"

"Just tell me."

"Okay, two and a half years ago. Why?"

"You remember hearing about Steve Hansen?"

"The name rings a bell, but I don't tie it to anything."

"Used to be a sergeant on this department. Killed his wife and daughter about three years back. Been on Death Row at Huntsville ever since they convicted him, playing the usual appeals games. You know how that goes."

"I know how that goes. What about him?"

"He escaped. About five-fifteen. Took off with a guard's gun and ID. They figure he's heading this way. He's dangerous as all hell. Shigata, you ain't gonna like this."

"I suppose I'm not. Give."

"He'd been talking a lot about escaping. That's why they had him loaded down with chain."

"Okay," Shigata said patiently. Quinn would tell his story his own way. He always did.

"He'd been saying he was gonna go to Bayport and kill the chief of police."

"Yippee. He doesn't even know me. Sure he doesn't mean somebody else?"

"He gets the Houston paper and the Galveston paper. He'd know."

"Who was it when he was arrested?" *Avoid saying anything to let Melissa know what was wrong, because she might start to worry.*

Start to worry. That was a joke. She never stopped worrying.

"Chief of police, you mean. Well, let's see. It was Shipp. Dale Shipp, and then he got demoted and then it was Cal Woodall and then Shipp again and then Buchanan and now you. Even me, come to think of it, for about a month after Buchanan bit the dust. I mean, this department has had a busy three years. He's got to have known. And he never did change his tune. It was always, he was gonna break out and go to Bayport and kill the chief of police."

"So how'd he make the break?"

Quinn explained.

"Thanks for letting me know," Shigata said resignedly.

"Your address isn't in the phone book and the dispatchers ain't giving it out," Quinn said unnecessarily. "But one like that, he'll always find out."

"Okay," Shigata said again. "We'll be on the lookout. There's not much else anybody can do. How're the roads?"

"Slicker'n owl shit."

"He's not going to get here tonight."

"Don't bet the rent on it."

Shigata waited. He knew Quinn well enough to know there was something else Quinn wanted to say but didn't want to say, something he found even more disturbing than the things he'd already said.

Which meant it was very, very bad. Al Quinn was a pragmatist.

"Shigata? What if I call you chief instead of boss?"

"Suit yourself."

"You know how you always say there's nobody more dangerous than a smart psychopath?"

"Yeah."

"Well, that's what I think he is. Hansen, I mean. I wasn't on the department then, but I knew him some. One night at this Fraternal Order of Police thing he got drunk, I mean *real* drunk, and started telling me his life story. He was one of these whiz kids, got out of high school at fourteen and went right into U.T., you know up there in Austin, and come out the other end with a Ph.D. before he was twenty-one. His daddy had his life all planned out for him, he was gonna be a Harvard professor time he was thirty and president of Yale time he was fifty. Then he turned twenty-one and said 'fuck you' to the old man and come down here and went on the police department making four hundred dollars a month. It took him years to learn to talk like other people. He used to sit around not quite drunk, just with a buzz on, and watch everybody else like we was insects under a magnifying glass. Funny guy but no harm in him, that's what I would have said then."

"What's his degree in?"

"English."

"You're kidding."

"I swear. I don't think I ever seen him but what he had a book stuck in his pocket. He'd always read while he was eating, and when he was reading, man, you could fire a shotgun over his head and he'd look up about five minutes later and say, 'What?' You know what he was reading during his trial? I was on the department by then."

"What was he reading?"

"Some real long poem called 'The Cenci.' He wanted to read it out loud to me one time and I told him to shut up. He was reading it over and over. And then he used to look at Shipp, and if I ever seen a man want to kill it was him."

Shigata whistled softly.

"That say something to you?"

"Maybe," Shigata said. "You say he killed his wife and daughter?"

"Yeah."

"How old was she? The daughter I mean."

"Fifteen, why?"

14

"I don't know. I want to think about it. Thanks for calling."

"Be careful, man."

"I'm always careful."

Threatened men live long. But Hansen sounded really dangerous.

$\triangledown$

Chapter 2

*I*IF IT'S NOT LOCKED. *If it's not locked.*

Where do you hide, in a town this size, where just about everybody knows you and you don't have a friend left?

Where do you hide something that you may not get back to for years, if ever?

He'd known from the start that he was going to be convicted. Even before he realized what must have really happened, it was simple. Gaylene was Shipp's daughter, and Shipp was going to burn somebody for her death. Hansen was the only somebody available.

But why did he need to burn me, if he really knew Lillian did it?

Did he hate me that much? If he did, when did he start hating me?

Or was it just that he was afraid I'd find out about him fathering Gaylene's baby?

There had to be a way Hansen could prove he hadn't done it without implicating Todd, but he couldn't—then—figure out what it was, and for that matter he still couldn't. For a while he was out on bond, a lot of bond. He'd put his house up (that was when he still had a house) to cover it. He didn't have a house now; the bank had foreclosed on it a long time ago. He'd known that would happen and there wasn't anything he could do about it. But if he ever got the chance to get back to town later, when things had quieted down . . .

He'd quietly sold everything he could think of to sell. Most of his guns; they'd seized only the one she'd been shot with. His car; lucky it was paid for clear. The television. He wouldn't have a chance to watch it again anyway. He'd come up with a thousand dollars, actually a little over a thousand dollars, by the time the bank foreclosed on the house.

The way the city was laid out, there were only two main downtown streets. That was all a town this size needed: a few city offices, a few stores. Mostly people went down to Galvez Plaza to shop, or up to one of the big malls between here and Houston.

The city offices were on one of those main streets. They took up one full block. Count 'em, left to right, like a row of tin soldiers: the fire department, with the little branch post office back to back with it. The police department with the little city courtroom. The water department, which also sold trash bags. The library. The mayor's office. And behind the mayor's office, behind the library, a dank windowless warehouse-looking area where old, dusty city records dating clear back before the turn of the century were stored.

You could reach that storage room from any one of several doors that led from the mayor's office, the library, the water department—even the police station. All those doors were kept locked.

But there was one door that was never locked, because the lock didn't work. The back door beside the post office, the back door that led to the alley. Hansen discovered that years ago and had properly reported it. The city was going to get it fixed.

Only nobody ever fixed it, and he didn't bother to report it again.

He'd stashed some things there, that last night when he was pretty sure they were going to lock him up again in the morning because there was no longer anything to back up his bond. All the money that was left: a thousand dollars in small bills, fives, tens, nothing larger than twenties. The

17

worn brown calfhide shoulder holster he wore when they had him in plain clothes, with the Colt detective special—blue steel, one-inch barrel with a hammer shroud so it wouldn't catch on your clothes when you drew from a shoulder holster. The revolver, and a box of ammo. A full box, because he wasn't sure how much he was going to need. An old billfold. A lot of change. A pocketknife. As much as he could manage of the usual paraphernalia men carry around in their pockets.

And keys. Not car keys, because he didn't have a car anymore, or house keys, because the bank had foreclosed on the house. He stored only the keys he expected to need again. The keys to the police station. The key to the newest patrol car, so that if it was still there when he got back—if he got back—he'd have short-term transportation.

Only short-term. They wouldn't let him live long enough to need long-term transportation.

A sleeping bag. Not the one he used on the beach, because he'd entered that, sandy as it was, into evidence, not that that did any good, because the DA had argued, perfectly reasonably, that sand on a sleeping bag didn't mean he was sleeping on the beach on any given night. No, this was Todd's sleeping bag. It would be dusty now, but he could shake the dust out.

If nobody had found it all, found it and turned it in or appropriated it. He'd taken all possible precautions against that, but no plan was perfect, especially when it had to be planned that quickly. So that was the big question, was any of it going to be still there. He'd slipped it into the top of a storage box labeled "City Tax Records 1919-1920." There shouldn't have been any reason for that box to be opened. That didn't mean it hadn't been.

He'd planned it all so carefully.

The idea then was to clear himself. It wasn't until the trial finally started that he'd realized Shipp had him sewed up tight. He'd never be able to clear himself, not without implicating Todd. Shipp had seen to that.

He'd never be able to clear himself, but he'd decided

during the trial, during those interminable years he'd sat on Death Row, that if he ever got the chance he'd use those preparations he'd made. He'd use them to kill Dale Shipp.

Because a man who'd deliberately convict another man—or a boy, if it came to that—of murder he knew hadn't happened the way he said it did—a man like that was too dangerous to live. Too dangerous, and too evil.

"Bayport exit, buddy."

He sat up. "Thanks a million."

"Any time. Don't give me a ticket next time you see me."

"Right." He forced the suggestion of a chuckle into his voice as he opened the door. This was the third trucker he'd ridden with tonight. None of them had asked questions; none of them had their CB's on. He couldn't stay this lucky forever. But now that didn't matter, because he didn't need another lift.

Two miles to the center of town, two miles with sleet dripping down his neck. He never stopped shivering. He used to work on nights like this, just like he did any other time, but he hadn't been out in the weather for three years. His head remembered what it felt like, but his body didn't.

I'd swap my left nut for a cup of coffee. Why not? I'm not doing anything with it anyway.

There were three black-and-whites parked in front of the police station, and for a moment a blaze of pure hatred threatened to swamp him. But he pushed it back down. He couldn't blame them for turning against him, just like he couldn't blame the jury for voting to convict him. He could see it just as well as they could, what it looked like.

And the other cops didn't think of him as one of them, because at best, even as a twenty-year veteran, he was an outsider. A hermit crab in a borrowed shell. A sheep in a wolf suit.

A motive—the quarrel, which wasn't really a motive at all, not a motive for him to kill Lillian and Gaylene, but enough murders had erupted out of domestic quarrels that he could see why it looked like a motive. An opportunity. Nobody had seen him between the time he left the bar at

19

midnight and the time he parked in front of his house at nine-thirty. His gun. His own damned service revolver, the Dan Wesson .357 with the five-inch barrel that he was supposed to carry with him all the time, only he didn't take it with him that night because he'd taken it off at home and forgot to put it back on before he left. He hadn't gone back for it because he'd had a hunch he was going to get very, very drunk before the night was over, and booze and guns don't mix so well.

And what did he have as an alibi?

I was asleep on the beach.

I didn't kill my wife and daughter.

They didn't even bother with autopsies, because Lillian's bullet had gone clean through and didn't have to be dug out to compare with the gun, and Gaylene's was so close to the surface that Buchanan dug it out with a pocketknife, for which the medical examiner's investigator shouted at him, but by then it was already done. Anyway, it was obvious what had killed them, and no autopsy was needed for that. And because there hadn't been an autopsy, he couldn't even say for sure—legally—that Gaylene was really pregnant. But whether she was or not it wouldn't have done him any good. They'd have said it was him did it to her.

The jury would believe it.

The other cops would believe it.

Men do molest their daughters, their stepdaughters, if they have no sense of decency at all and the wife is getting old and fat while the daughter is getting prettier and prettier.

And Gaylene was way the hell and gone the other side of pretty.

Tamar. Tamar. Tamar. Girl, what the hell did we do to you, all of us together, letting you run around with those short skirts and that long hair?

The door opened with a little bit of a creak, not enough to be heard through the storage room and into the other parts of the building. Nobody would be in any of it anyway, except the police department and the fire department, and the firemen mostly would be asleep. There shouldn't be more

20

than four people in the police station, and they were on the front side of the building.

If Shipp was there he could do it now and get away, still have a chance to talk to Todd. But catch Dale Shipp working on a night like this.

It was warm and dusty; the steam pipes ran through this room and he could hear a little bit of water dripping—oh yes, that sink in the corner. A janitor's sink that the janitor never never used because there were more convenient janitor's sinks in other parts of the building.

He turned on the sixty-watt overhead light. There weren't any windows. Nobody would know he was there.

Thank God. It was warm water dripping, and he held his freezing hands under the drip. Then he stopped long enough to take off his jacket. He was warmer with it off. Not much, but a little.

He thrust his hands back under the warm water, until finally he stopped shaking. Then he went over to the box to check.

It hadn't been opened, it hadn't been moved, and the top of the box had kept the dust out. The sleeping bag was clean. The gun was dry, still gleaming with the oil from the last night he'd methodically cleaned it before he stored it here.

He took Rusty Claiborne's gunbelt off, took the wallet out of his pocket, and stuck an extra twenty in it. Claiborne wouldn't report that, if he even happened to notice it, which he probably wouldn't. Then silently, using the point of his pocket knife blade, he slipped the lock into the city hall.

It was empty, just as it should be this time of night. He knew the way to the mailroom.

He located a box that looked right to hold everything he'd taken from Rusty Claiborne. After filling the box, he wrapped it neatly, addressed it to Rusty Claiborne at Huntsville State Prison, and used the city postage meter on it. He put a ten-dollar bill on the table beside the postage meter. *I'm not a thief. You can send me to prison, but you can't make me steal.*

Now what? If he left it here, somebody would certainly notice.

He couldn't relock the door, but nobody would notice that the next time they came to open it. They'd just swear a little and turn the key a few more times.

Back out the door to the street. The post office is never locked; people might want to come in and check their boxes even if the road is a sheet of ice.

He dropped the package into the mail chute.

They'll call me crazy. Well, maybe I am. But I'm not a thief. Dear God, I'm not a thief.

Tomorrow's Saturday. They won't be using city hall. I can sleep a little late. Well, I've got to sleep a little late, before I go look for Todd.

He knew where Todd was. He'd written a lot of letters. He hadn't gotten any reply except that one that wasn't really a reply at all, but he could understand that.

He filled his empty belly with water from the dripping faucet and then dragged the sleeping bag back behind a stack of boxes and lay down in it.

He thought he wouldn't sleep.

But he did.

∇

Chapter 3

SHIGATA ENTERED HIS OFFICE at 5:00 A.M. to find Quinn sitting at his desk writing. Quinn closed the notebook, not too quickly for Shigata to see a page full of numbers. "Still working on that problem?"

"It's still my problem," Quinn said flatly.

"Sorry, I'm not trying to pry. But if a loan would help—"

"It wouldn't." Belatedly, Quinn added, "Thanks. Anyway, you're as broke as I am."

"Not quite."

"Close enough it doesn't matter. I pulled his personnel file for you."

Shigata, slightly foggy from the hour and Quinn's abrupt change of subject, asked, "Whose personnel file?"

"Hansen's. I think you'll find it interesting."

"Meaning, you read it."

"Sure I read it. I've got to do something to stay awake in the middle of the night, don't I? Besides play with numbers, I mean."

"Right," Shigata said. "And don't come in tonight. You're dead on your feet."

"What do you plan on doing? Doubling over twice when you need to be especially alert?"

"No, I've had a better idea," Shigata said. "I'm going to

create a couple of acting corporals—no pay differential, I'd have to go through city council to get that—but they'll be serving as watch commanders with orders to call one of us for anything bigger than a fender bender or dog bite. It'll get them some good experience and let you and me get some rest."

"So who do you have in mind?"

"Barlow and Barndt, that sound okay to you? Barlow for swing, Barndt for deep nights."

"Ted's young."

"I know he's young, but he's got a lot of street smart."

"And his daddy used to be your boss."

"That doesn't have anything to do with it, and you know it."

"And I'll bet you money Barndt's gone to a bigger department inside of six months."

"I'm not so sure about that. She did cut her hair without my having to tell her to."

"After you dropped hints the size of elephants," Quinn said, and yawned widely.

"Why don't you go home?"

"I'm going, I'm going."

Of course he wasn't going; he spent another half hour methodically putting things away and getting things ready, but Shigata settled down to read the personnel report.

His first thought was, Hansen didn't sound like a flake.

To be sure, he'd worked for the department twenty years and never gotten a higher rank than sergeant, with all the turnover. That could say several things. It could say he was stupid, which he was not. Or it could say he was incompetent, but his file contained absolutely no indication of incompetence. Or it could say he lacked ambition, which was hard to believe of somebody who had a Ph.D. before he was twenty-one. Or it could say he was the perpetual outsider. And that was what Shigata was inclined to believe.

His file contained no reports of misconduct. He'd never been accused of unnecessarily roughing up a prisoner, of improper use of firearms, or even of being late to work or

24

inappropriately absent. From what Quinn had said, Hansen might have a little bit of a drinking problem, but you couldn't tell it from this file. His quarterly reports had always been good, never outstanding but never bad.

He didn't, from this file—from the black-and-white photograph of a young Steve Hansen grinning from the page—look like a man who would flip out and kill his wife and daughter, a man who might even now be stalking Shigata. *I don't want to have to kill this man,* he thought.

Quinn, jacket on, stepped back into the office. "What do you think?"

"I thought you went home."

"About Hansen."

Shigata shook his head. "I don't see anything."

"Neither did I. And maybe that's something."

"Meaning?"

"Meaning Dale Shipp was chief of police when Hansen flipped out."

Shigata considered, nodded. "We might better have a look at the case file. Where would it be?"

"Storeroom. Back in the far west corner. You remember last month when the clerk of the court gave us back all that stuff?"

"I remember distinctly," Shigata said. A new clerk of the court and a new D.A.'s secretary, housecleaning simultaneously, had returned to the local police departments evidence and prosecution files from approximately ten years' worth of felony trials. Shigata had returned the valuables to their owners, jammed firearms and narcotics into the safe behind his desk until he had time to think about them, and told Quinn to find a place to park the paperwork.

"Well, it was part of that," Quinn said.

"Okay, I'll look for it later. I'm going to hit the road now."

In a department this size, even the chief patrolled at the busier times of day.

Hansen slipped back into the city offices. It was more dangerous this time, in broad daylight at nine in the morning. But the sky was still overcast; nobody was on the sidewalk to watch him slither on hands and knees, below the windowsill, to the first telephone he could reach.

Dial 9 to get out. Standard procedure anywhere.

But he couldn't remember the number. He pulled the phone book out onto the floor. Morgan's Accounting Services; he'd called it plenty of times, but that was three years ago. Shelley Morgan. Lillian's sister. Lillian's baby sister. She'd always acted as if he crawled out of the gutter, as if he were too stupid (with all his degrees) to get a better job than he had. She never could understand that he *wanted* the job he had.

And maybe it was part jealousy. Lillian had him—Lillian, fat and plain, and it would be false modesty to say he wasn't a good-looking man. Lillian had him. Shelley, who was younger and slim and always kept herself looking nice, had made a pass at him once. Just once, at a Christmas party, so she could always claim later (if he mentioned it later) that it was the booze, not her. But of course he didn't mention it later. He'd said all he was going to when it happened. He'd said, "I love Lillian. I love my wife. And I'm an honest man. Go hunt somebody else. I'm taken."

She'd always believed he did kill Lillian and Gaylene. Or at least she claimed to believe it. She hadn't helped him in court, that was for sure. She testified she'd seen him hit Lillian, and that was a lie, he'd never hit Lillian. But Lillian wasn't there to testify, and nobody was going to believe him.

She had another reason to hate him now. The court gave her custody of Todd. She didn't want Todd, but she took him because she saw it as her duty.

That gave Hansen cold chills. He'd thought then, and still thought now, God help any kid who's given a home because it's somebody's duty. He'd just about be better off on the street.

Hansen even suspected she was hiding his letters to Todd, when he didn't get any answer, until he fired off an angry letter to her and got a reply from Todd. The only letter he'd ever had from Todd.

26

No salutation.
Just the careful handwriting.

Aunt Shelley wanted me to tell you she is not taking
the letters you write me. I get them. I just don't want
to read them.
Todd.

How much of that was Todd and how much was Shelley?
With luck, he'd find out soon.
He dialed. The phone rang four times. Then the same
crisp voice; Shelley always sounded at least halfway angry.
"Morgan's Accounting Services. Hello? Hello?"
She hung up before he had the chance.
Then the other number.
Todd answered, an insecure voice in the process of changing.
And once again, Steve Hansen hung up without speaking.
He slithered back into the storage room, closing the door
carefully again, wishing he'd thought to stash some clothes
in here. But at least he was in denim, not prison coveralls.
He wouldn't be that conspicuous. Not unless he ran into
somebody he knew.
If that happened, it would just be the breaks. He'd made
up his mind to that. He was going to kill Dale Shipp. He
wasn't going to kill anybody else. And if he missed Shipp,
well, he missed.
The rain and sleet had stopped, and it was back above
freezing. The roads were still slick, but, if he stayed off the
sidewalk or the street and walked on the frost-blackened
grass, he didn't fall very often.
Three-quarters of a mile. Distances aren't so great, in a
town this size, that you can't get by without a car.
If Shelley still lived in the same place. He hadn't thought
to check on that.
Still the same fifties-style tract house, faded green asbes-
tos siding, a carport with wrought-iron posts once white,
now rusting. "Morgan" in white on the mailbox. She still
lived here.
He paused for a moment just inside the carport, listening.

He didn't figure she'd have gotten a dog. Not Shelley; she hated dogs, even if Todd did love them. But just in case—

No barking.

The TV was on. "Teenage Mutant Ninja Turtles." Anybody ought to get a special award for dreaming up a title like that.

Soundlessly—he'd always been able to move soundlessly—he eased closer to the door, looked through the glass.

Todd was in his underwear, stained jockey shorts and a white T-shirt. He was sprawled on the couch in a nest of comic books, with a bowl of potato chips and a two-liter bottle of Coke in front of him.

Hansen eased the door open.

Todd didn't turn around. The way the house was laid out, the door opened into the kitchen, but there wasn't a wall between the kitchen and the living room. Shelley had used a couch as a space divider. So Todd had his back to the kitchen and the door, facing directly away from Hansen.

Hansen let the door close a little more loudly.

Todd still didn't turn around. But Hansen had seen the slight movement that told him Todd heard him come in. Heard him, and thought he was Shelley, and knew Shelley was going to yell at him for not being dressed, for making a mess in the living room. Knew it, and didn't care.

"That's not much of a breakfast, son." he said softly.

Todd sat up and spun around in one movement, and Hansen saw unmistakable fear on the boy's face.

"It's just me, Todd." He held his arms out, clear of his sides, so Todd could see his hands were empty.

"I figured you'd come here. They said on TV you broke out. What do you want?" His voice was almost through changing. Deep. He was going to be—almost was—a baritone.

"To talk with you."

"Like you talked with Mom and Gaylene?"

"I didn't do that, Todd."

"Everybody else says you did."

"Everybody else is wrong."

28

Deliberately, Todd reached for the telephone on the round end table beside the couch. Then he paused. "Aren't you going to stop me?"

"No. If you want to turn me in, go ahead. I don't promise to stay here if you do, but I won't stop you."

Todd sat, indecisive, and then took his hand off the phone. "I guess I won't right now."

"Thanks. Is it okay if I sit down?"

"Yeah. I guess."

"Mind if I have some of those chips?"

"You said it wasn't much of a breakfast."

"It isn't. But it's better than nothing. I haven't had anything to eat since noon yesterday, and I'm pretty hungry."

"Why didn't you just rob a store?"

"Because I'm not a robber."

"No, just a killer."

"Do you really believe that?"

"Why shouldn't I?"

"You lived with me thirteen years," Hansen said. "Did I ever hit you? Did you ever see me hit Gaylene, or your mother?"

"No, but—"

"But what?"

"But you always had a gun."

"Todd, I was a police officer. I had to have a gun."

"How many people did you shoot?"

"I never shot anybody. I never wanted to shoot anybody."

"Are you a police officer now?"

"You know I'm not."

"But I bet you have a gun."

"You win that one. I have a gun."

"Who are you going to shoot?" At Hansen's silence, Todd said triumphantly, "You can't answer that, can you? You are going to shoot somebody. I knew it. Who are you going to shoot? Me?"

"No. Not you."

"Shelley?"

29

"No. I don't like Shelley, but that's no reason to kill her."

"Who, then?"

"Nobody you know."

"Then why'd you come here?"

"Because I wanted to see you. Because I wanted to tell you the truth."

"People who tell the truth don't need guns."

Hansen had to laugh. "Who told you that? Shelley? It sounds like something Shelley would say. I'll tell you what . . . I'll take the gun off, and then—" He stopped abruptly. As his hand moved toward the shoulder holster, the fear was back in Todd's face.

Hansen put his hands on top of his head. "You get the gun," he said. "Put it on top of the TV."

"I don't like guns."

"I don't blame you. But you've got three choices—either I keep on wearing the gun, or I take it off, or you take it off me. Which is it?"

"I don't care. You might as well go on wearing it. If you wanted it you'd get it anyway, even if it was on top of the TV."

"Todd, have you looked in a mirror lately?"

"What's that supposed to mean?"

"It means you're two inches taller than I am and forty pounds heavier. There's no way I could get past you unarmed, even if I did want to. Stand up again. Let me get a good look at you. How long have you been shaving?"

"Not long."

"You don't want to talk to me, do you?"

"No. I don't want to talk to you."

"You like living with Shelley?"

"No. But there's nowhere else to live. Shelley tried to send me to your dad, but he wouldn't take me. Whey does *he* hate you? What did you do to *him*?"

"You wouldn't understand."

"I probably wouldn't."

"Will you get me a glass of water?" Hansen asked.

"Get your own water."

"The front window is open. I don't want anybody to see me here."

"Then get it in the bathroom. You know where it is."

"Right. I know where it is." He didn't move from the couch for a moment. Then he got up and walked to the bathroom and deliberately closed the door. *This isn't going the way I had planned. I should have known it wouldn't. Well, he's got his chance now. Let him turn me in if he wants to. I don't guess I'll fight.* He ran water into his cupped hands, drank, used the toilet, flushed noisily, and returned to the living room.

From all he could see, Todd hadn't moved. He was still sitting on the couch, his eyes fixed on the TV screen, his hand in the potato-chip bowl.

"Does it make you feel better to ignore me?"

"It'd make me feel better if you'd go away."

"I'll go away pretty soon. Todd, please listen to me now. This is probably the last time you'll ever see me—the last time I'll ever see you. That doesn't matter to you now, or at least you say it doesn't. But it matters a lot to me, and God willing, someday it will matter to you."

"If you didn't kill them, who did?"

"I don't know. I'm leaning to the notion Lillian did it herself."

"She wouldn't do that!"

"She wouldn't, but I would?"

Todd just looked at him, his young face sullen.

Hansen shrugged. "You got a job?"

"No."

"What kind of grades are you making?"

"I'm passing."

"That all?"

"Time you were my age you were in college, right?"

"Right," Hansen said. "But that doesn't mean I expect you to—"

"What good did they ever do you, all those degrees?"

"Depends on what you mean by good. I like learning."

"Gladly would he learn and gladly teach?"

31

"So the boy is literate after all. No, Todd, gladly would I learn, but I didn't have the slightest interest in teaching."

Todd sat up straight and looked at him, really looked at him for the first time. "Were you screwing Gaylene?"

"No, I was not. What made you ask that?"

"Shelley said you were screwing Gaylene. Course, she put it a lot nicer. She said you were screwing Gaylene and Mom found out and that's why you shot them. And you didn't shoot me because I was your kid and Gaylene wasn't."

Hansen got up, walked without hurry to the bathroom, leaned over the toilet, and vomited the water he'd drunk. He kept on retching despite an empty stomach, until finally it was over and he sat down rather limply on the bathroom floor.

"Why'd you do that?" Todd asked from the bathroom door, with no more than mild interest.

"I don't know. Maybe it's what I think of a man who'd screw his own daughter. Maybe it's what I think of my son thinking I'm that kind of man."

"Gaylene wasn't your daughter."

"Who told you that? Shelley again?" He sat up straight. "No. Gaylene wasn't my daughter in the sense that I shot off the right load of sperm at the right time. If that's how you think of it. If that's what being a father means to you. You ever jack off? You ever lay a girl? You're sixteen now, you ever lay a girl?"

"Yeah. I laid a girl. So what?"

"She get pregnant?"

"No."

"How do you know?"

"She'd have told me if she did."

"S'pose she didn't tell you. Suppose she went off somewhere and had the baby and gave it up for adoption. Then who'd be the father? You? Or the guy that raises her? Use your head, kid. Screwing doesn't make a man a father. Raising a kid makes a man a father. I raised Gaylene. In every way that matters to me, I was her father. No. I didn't screw Gaylene. But I think somebody did, and I think that's why she and Lillian are dead, and if I can find the man that did it, well, Todd, that's the man I'm going to kill."

"Because he screwed Gaylene? You're gonna kill a man for screwing Gaylene? Because if you are, you're gonna be busy. Gaylene was screwing half the football team."

"Do you know that?"

"Well, I—"

"Do you know that? Or is it just what somebody told you? Because that's a hell of a thing for you to go around saying about your own sister."

"I don't say it. They say it to me."

"Who says it to you?"

"People."

"Who?"

"You gonna kill them too?"

"No. I just want to know who's saying it."

"Different people. Different times. No. I don't know it. I don't think she was. Not really. Somebody was screwing her, though, because she was pregnant. And I do know that."

"How do you know?"

Silence.

"I asked you a question. How do you know?"

"You and Mom had your own bathroom. Gaylene and I used the other bathroom. She—kinda left things lying around. Things that she should have put in the trash. Only she hadn't left any lying around for the last couple of months. And she was barfing in the morning and she was barfing in the afternoon and one day I asked her what was wrong and she said nothing was wrong and then Mom came in and asked her what was wrong and she started crying and crying and crying. Somebody was screwing her. And it was somebody she didn't want to screw her."

Hansen took a deep breath. "That's what I thought."

"You know who it was?"

"I'm pretty sure I do."

"Anyway, why would you want to kill somebody just for making Gaylene pregnant? That doesn't make sense."

"It doesn't unless whoever made her pregnant also killed

her," Hansen said softly. "Killed her and Lillian both." *Not in the sense of pulling the trigger. But just as sure as if he had.*

"I thought you said Mom—"

"Did it. Yes. But if somebody made her want to—"

"That's what you think happened?"

Hansen nodded.

"Thinking doesn't make it true. You used to tell me that."

"That's true. I did."

"I still don't know it wasn't you."

"No. I know you don't, son."

"Are you gonna sit on the bathroom floor all day?"

"No, I'm getting up now."

"Because it's eleven-thirty and Shelley usually comes home about noon on Saturday."

"Thanks for telling me."

"I still don't believe you," Todd said.

"Do you want to?"

A long silence. "Yes. I guess I want to."

"Thanks for that, anyway. Will you give me some of that Coke?"

"Take all of it. You need any money? I've got a little."

"What?"

"Thanks. I stashed some away. Todd."

"I'd like to give you a hug."

"No."

Hansen stood up. "Okay. I can understand. I'm going now. Just—remember I love you."

"Dad—" Todd stopped, face flushed. "That's the first time I've called you that in three years."

"I know."

"I can give you my last year's jacket. I outgrew it anyway."

"Thanks. But I better not take it."

"Because it's mine?"

"Because it's yours. I don't want anybody to realize, later, that you must have given it to me."

"What if you kill the guy you think it is and he didn't do it?"

"I'll be sure before I pull the trigger." *I'm sure now. But I can't make you understand that, and I'm not going to try.*

34

"What happens after you kill whoever it is?"

"Maybe I go back to prison. Maybe I don't."

"You mean they might kill you?"

"They might."

"Doesn't that scare you?"

"Dying? Not much. Everybody dies sometime. If I stay in prison, sooner or later they'll kill me there. What difference does it make where or how they kill me? Whatever happens will embarrass you. I'm sorry about that, but there's nothing I can do about it."

"Except not kill whoever it is. Keep on running. I mean— why do you want to kill him? What good will it do? It won't brin$_\downarrow$ back Mom or Gaylene."

"It might keep him from doing to somebody else's family what he's done to ours."

"Dad, Mom wouldn't have done it. She wouldn't. I know she wouldn't—not kill herself and Gaylene and leave me alive in this sort of mess."

Hansen didn't answer. But he was thinking, a blond boy and a blond dog in a sleeping bag, on the front porch because it was just about too hot to sleep indoors and on his salary he couldn't pay for air conditioning. The middle of a moonlit night. No lights. A blond dog shot in the head.

Why shoot the dog?

By mistake, thinking the dog's head was the boy's head?

But who would have fired those shots?

"Where did you go that night?" he asked abruptly.

"How do you know I went anywhere?"

"Don't give me that shit. Three shots fired, one of them right beside your head, and you slept right through it? No way. I don't care how much codeine you took. Where did you go that night?"

"I went to the pool hall. I didn't want to listen to you and Mom fight."

"At thirteen they let you into the pool hall?"

"There were a lot of people in there. They didn't notice me."

"You and I both know that's a load of crap. Let me make a guess. You sneaked off with Ted Zimmer to smoke a little pot and you didn't want to come home till your eyes were clear. Then you sneaked back home and found the house dark. Honey was already in the sleeping bag and you were still half stoned on top of the codeine, so you crawled in there too and didn't notice till morning that Honey was dead."

"How'd you know I'd been smoking pot?"

"I've got a nose," Hansen said.

"Then why didn't you do anything about it?"

"I was trying to find out who you and Ted were getting it from. Then I was going to put his ass under the jail. That's what happened, isn't it?"

"Yeah."

"You still smoke pot?"

"No. Not since then. Would it have helped you if I'd said that at your trial?"

"Probably not. So don't worry about it."

After a moment, Todd asked, "So if it wasn't Mom and it wasn't you—what if it was him?"

"Him who? The guy that was selling you pot?"

"No, that was just a guy at school. Him—whoever it was, the guy that was screwing Gaylene. Is he—if you know who it is, is he a person that would do that? Kill Mom and Gaylene and Honey?"

"Maybe. I think so." *I think so. Especially if he thought Honey was you. Because Honey wouldn't bark at Shipp. She knew him. And she was an old dog anyway; she'd just about quit barking.*

But if Shipp did do it, why did he look the way he looked that morning? I'm sure he really thought it was me—then.

There's something there I don't understand. But Shipp's in it somewhere, somehow. Fugue state? Maybe he did it and then blanked out on it until he was calmer?

Damn it, who did it, if it wasn't Lillian and it wasn't me and it wasn't Todd and it wasn't Shipp (but Shipp knew, later), who could it have been?

It must have been Lillian. Lillian, but Shipp drove her to it, and he's as responsible as if he pulled the trigger himself.

"Then couldn't you prove it?" Todd was demanding. "If

it was somebody else, couldn't you prove it? Then you wouldn't—" Todd stopped.

Hansen was shaking his head. "No," he said. "No, if there was a way I could have proved it once, he'll have made sure I can't do it now."

"You'd better go now."

"Yeah." Hansen moved toward the door.

"Dad?"

"Yeah?"

"I'll shake hands. And—and if you go back to prison, I'll write. Daddy? Please don't get killed. Please don't. Please don't."

"I'll do my best not to." *That's the only lie I've ever told you, the only lie I ever will tell you. Good-bye, my son. May you have a better life than your daddy ever did.*

He paused at the kitchen door and looked back, seeing Todd standing by the couch, his throat moving convulsively. *I don't want to leave him crying, and I've got to go.* "Kid," Hansen said, "will you take a little advice from your old man?"

"Maybe."

"You'd be better off keeping your fly zipped a few more years. But if you're going to do it, use a condom."

Todd looked at him, his face completely startled.

"And put some pants on before your aunt gets home. It's indecent to run around in front of her in your underwear."

"That's what she says."

"Yeah, well, every now and then I agree with her. Take care, son."

"Yeah. Bye."

Todd stood for a moment and then headed down the hall. Hansen let the door ease shut behind him.

He was at the corner when Shelley drove by.

He saw her.

She didn't see him.

He'd done one of the two things on his list. He'd seen Todd. And if Todd still didn't believe him—and he didn't,

37

Hansen was sure of that—at least he was a little more willing to try to believe him.

He was ready to do the other now. To kill Shipp. And he knew that Shipp often hung around the police station on Saturday afternoon, but—well—he wasn't ready yet. Not as ready as he'd thought only moments ago he was.

As composedly as if he didn't know that his picture was on the front page of the Houston and Galveston papers, he walked to the closest 7-Eleven, pausing only long enough outside to look through the glass and see to it there was no one he knew inside. Then he went in and bought a sandwich, a quart of milk, and a pair of shoelaces, eyeing the newspaper carefully as he waited for change. At least his picture wasn't above the fold; nobody was going to pause at this counter, look at him, dive for a telephone.

He stood outside, ate the sandwich and drank the milk, stuffed the trash into the trash can, and then put first one foot and then the other up on the ledge below the window glass, to insert and tie the shoelaces. When he finished he walked toward I-45.

Get caught hitching on I-45 in the daylight and I'll be right back inside. But it's okay to hitch on the entrance ramps. And hope like hell no cop car comes along.

It took him thirty-five minutes to get to the end of the highway.

There were a couple of things he ought to do before he went down to walk on the beach. There used to be a Goodwill a couple of blocks away. . . .

It was still there. And there were still a few jackets left from winter, dust on their ragged sleeves, a half-price sticker across the original two-dollar price tag.

A yellow nylon jacket with royal blue stripes across the sleeves. A long-sleeved red plaid shirt.

A laundromat across the street, with a restroom in it. He locked the door carefully, took off the prison jacket, the shoulder holster, the prison shirt. He put the plaid shirt on, and the shoulder holster, and the nylon jacket. The jacket was about two sizes too big; the holster couldn't be seen even by somebody looking for it.

He put the denim shirt and the jacket into the bag the other clothes had been in, walked back across the street, and stuffed it into the Goodwill collection bin. With reasonable luck, they wouldn't be found until much later in the day. With good luck, nobody would notice the Huntsville State Prison stamp inside them until after they were washed and ready to be priced.

Then, as casually as a free man on his own legal business, he walked back down to the seawall and stood on it, gazing out to sea. The gulls were wheeling and crying raucously. Not many people were on the beach today; it was too cold. Far too cold to swim, not that he wanted to. Just to walk on the beach. Just to smell the ocean and watch the waves and the gulls—*Lillian loved the beach*—his throat ached.

Someone was standing beside him. He looked down, not to the side. Down at a pair of polished brown shoes, at the cuffs of light-brown knife-pleated trousers. *Uh-oh. Deputy sheriff.*

He didn't move. He didn't look to the side. He stayed exactly where he was, gazing out to sea, concentrating on keeping his breathing even. *Don't look at my face, brother. Don't look at my face, because if you do one of us is going to die on this seawall. Most likely me, because I've got nothing against you.* After a while the deputy said, "Nice weather, after all that crud yesterday."

"Yeah," Hansen said.

"Where you from?"

"Dallas." He made it sound like "Dallis." The lookouts might have mentioned his educated speech pattern. Not that there was much left of it now.

"That's a hell of a place to have to stay," the deputy said. "I go up there about once in three years. I don't see how you can breathe there."

"It ain't always easy," Hansen said. "Better down here."

"Yeah. I've lived here all my life. You couldn't pay me to leave. Well, have a nice weekend."

Hansen stood, unmoving, until he heard the deputy's

footsteps retreating in the distance. Then, still without haste, he walked down the staircase from the seawall to the beach. Still without haste, he walked up the beach to the next staircase. *That was close. I guess I've got to get back indoors.*

The far west corner of the storage room. Shigata found the case file without much trouble.

He wasn't looking for the sleeping bag, in the far east corner of the room. So, of course, he didn't see it.

Hansen didn't leave the beach after all. He wasn't ready to go quite yet, deputy or no deputy. He walked back down the stairs and sat down on a large stone. After a while, he wept.

It was after midnight when Todd Hansen called to report that the aunt he lived with was twelve hours late getting home from work, so it was Claire Barndt who got the call first.

After she found out who he was, she called Mark Shigata.

Chapter 4

THE BOY WAS BIG. That was Shigata's first thought when he stepped inside the house. Probably six-four, at least two hundred pounds and maybe more. Part of it was muscle; a little too much—for a kid this age—was fat. Blond and blue-eyed, he looked like a person who would be named Hansen. A big blond Viking of a kid. He made Shigata, at five-ten, feel small.

He didn't look quite healthy, and he did look scared. More scared even than this situation should call for.

Shigata introduced himself, and the kid nodded.

"Officer Barndt told me what's going on," Shigata said, "but I want to be sure I've got it right. So interrupt me if there's anything I've got wrong. Your aunt is Shelley Morgan?"

The kid nodded.

"And she runs Morgan's Accounting Services? That's just a couple of blocks from city hall, right?"

The kid nodded again, and then said, "Yeah. That's right."

"And you were expecting her home at noon. She didn't show up. What time did you call her office?"

"I guess about three-thirty."

"Why no sooner than that?"

"Because sometimes she's late."

41

"And she didn't answer the phone. And you haven't seen or heard from her since."

"Right."

"So you called the police station a little after midnight, to ask the officers to check her office."

"Yeah."

"And Officer Barndt checked the office and then came out here to talk with you." Shigata paused. "You seen your dad lately?"

The kid swallowed convulsively and said, "No." He wasn't looking at Shigata. He was looking past him, at the window from the living room into the garage.

"You're lying," Shigata said very softly. "Son, I can understand you not wanting to sell out your dad. I'm not asking you to. I just need to get things straight in my head. You and I both know your dad's on the street, and this would be one of the first places he would come. I would have had an officer here all day, but I didn't know where you were living and couldn't get hold of the right people to ask until Monday. What time did your aunt leave this morning?"

"About nine."

"What time did your dad get here?"

Silence.

"What time did your dad get here?"

More silence. Shigata simply waited. Sooner or later, the silence would unnerve the boy and he'd start talking.

It took about five minutes, while the boy's hands twisted a loose turning on the arm of the couch back and forth, back and forth. The turning squeaked, and the boy looked down at it blindly. Finally he spoke. "About eleven-fifteen. I think he called about nine-forty-five. I got a phone call, and there was nobody there."

"What time did he leave?"

"About eleven-forty-five."

"He didn't stay long. How come?"

"I didn't want him to. Anyway, I didn't want Shelley to see him."

"How do your dad and Shelley get along?"

42

Brief silence. Then: "Not very well. But he wouldn't hurt her. He told me so."

"What was your dad wearing?"

"Jeans. Chambray shirt. Denim jacket."

"Prison issue?"

"I guess. I didn't ask. It just looked like the kind of thing he always wore at home."

"What was he driving?"

"He was walking."

"He left here at eleven-forty-five walking, and Shelley was due home about noon. If she saw him, do you think she'd stop?"

"No. She'd more likely try to run over him."

Shigata glanced at the shadowed face. No. The boy hadn't meant it a as joke.

"Is your dad armed?"

"Yes." No hesitation on that one.

"Did he tell you why?"

"He said he was gonna kill somebody. But he wouldn't tell me who. He said it wasn't Shelley."

"You asked?"

"Yes. I asked. I even asked if it was me. Wouldn't you ask, if you were me?"

"I probably would. Did he say why he wanted to kill whoever it was?"

"Yes." The voice was almost inaudible.

"Why?"

"For screwing around with my sister."

"Son, your sister's dead."

"Stop calling me son. I'm not your son. And I know my sister's dead and my mother's dead and now you want to kill my father and you want me to help you do it and I'm not going to. I don't know where my dad is. He didn't hurt Shelley. He wouldn't. If he was going to hurt Shelley, he would have done it a long time ago. And I don't believe it was him killed my mom and my sister. He wouldn't. Shelley lied in court. Shelley said she saw him hit my mom, and she didn't. She couldn't have, because he never did hit my mom. And he never did hit my sister and he never did hit me. I

43

know a lot of guys' dads hit them but my dad didn't. Not ever. I don't know where Shelley is and I'm scared, but I'm not scared about my dad. Don't tell me my sister's dead. I know my sister's dead. You stupid cops, you couldn't find out who did it so you said Dad did because that was easy, he was there and they had a fight and I lied in court too, I said he didn't go anywhere that night but I didn't really know if he did or not because I left. I went to sleep because of the codeine, but then I woke up and Mom was still crying and I sneaked off and when I got back everything was quiet and I thought they'd all gone to bed but they hadn't, and I didn't see him again until he drove up that morning and that was after Mom and Gaylene were already dead. I think he did leave. A lot of times when he and Mom were having a fight he'd leave, and then he'd come back when he got through being mad and they'd sit down and watch TV and kiss a lot. He didn't do it. He left and somebody else came and did it. Not him. Not my dad. Shelley kept telling me he did it and she made me believe it and—and—until I saw him today and he was just the same only he was scared, I never saw him scared before—They're going to kill him for doing it and he didn't do it. He didn't do it. He didn't—"

The boy stopped. He was out of breath, and he was crying. He sat down hard on the couch, hiding his face so nobody could see him cry.

"Okay," Shigata said.

The boy looked up. "That's all you're going to say? Just okay?"

"What else do you want me to say?"

"I don't know."

"Can you tell me about Shelley's car?"

"It's just a car."

"Make? Model? License number?"

"Can't you get that off a computer or something?"

"Yes, but it will be faster if you tell us."

"It's a green Mercury Cougar. About ten years old." He gave the license number. "I'm not a hundred percent sure about the year."

"That's enough for us to go on."

"What are you going to do now?"

"Try to find Shelley."

"And my dad?"

"Him too."

"What are you going to do when you find him? Are you going to kill him?"

"I hope not. I don't like to kill people."

"Did you ever kill anybody?"

"Yes."

"How did you feel about it?"

"Awful."

"Why? I meant why did you do it, if it made you feel awful?"

"Because he was trying to kill me. He'd already killed my wife and one of her sisters."

"Did you want to kill him for that?"

"No. I just wanted to catch him. But when he saw me, he started shooting."

"My dad won't shoot at you."

"If he doesn't, then I'll have no cause to shoot at him."

"My dad doesn't even really want to kill whoever it is he wants to kill." The boy stopped, apparently replaying that sentence in his head. "That doesn't make much sense, does it?"

"I think I know what you mean. Did he tell you that?"

"No. But I could tell."

"Anything else you want to tell me?"

"No."

"Okay." Shigata stood up. "We'll leave an officer with you the rest of the night."

"What for?"

"Just in case."

"In case my dad comes back?"

"I wasn't thinking about that," Shigata said.

"I don't want an officer here."

"Then the officer will stay outside. But I've got to leave one here. Claire."

"Sir?"

"Can you take care of that?"

"I thought you would."

"You're watch commander."

She blushed slightly and said, "Yes, sir." She picked up the walkie-talkie she'd laid on the table. "Thirteen to headquarters."

"Headquarters, go ahead."

"Can you get—um—Ames over here to my location?"

"Ten-four. Headquarters to Ames—"

Claire Barndt put the radio back on the table. Shigata sat down again. "Todd, please believe me. I do not want to harm your dad. I'm not trying to trap him. I hope you're right that he's innocent. If he is, I'll help him all I can. But right now he's legally an escapee and he's legally armed and dangerous. We've got to assume he is in fact armed and dangerous. But that doesn't mean we'll shoot first and ask questions later."

"Okay." The muffled voice didn't sound okay. The boy was crying again.

Shigata waited until he was in the Bronco to call headquarters and put a lookout on the car. The he went on into the station. It was two A.M. There was no use trying for any sleep tonight.

It doesn't take long to rearrange the Ten Most Wanted list. As of six o' clock Sunday morning, when FBI agent Jim Barlow—the special agent in charge of the Houston office—stormed into the Bayport Police Department, Steven Hansen was on that list.

That was after a Texas City patrol officer found Shelley Morgan's car at five A.M. parked on Bexar Street where it formed a border between Texas City and Bayport. Shelley wasn't in it. A lot of blood was.

"You're hiding him," Barlow charged.

"I'm doing what?" Shigata asked blankly.

"You're hiding Steve Hansen."

"Would you like to explain to me why I would be hiding Steve Hansen?" Shigata asked politely. "Or have you forgotten

46

that the last word I got was, he wanted to kill me?"

"Because you're a stupid, quixotic son of a bitch."

"Thanks a lot."

"Look at you! You know you were the first Nisei on the Bureau?"

"I'm not Nisei. That means first generation out of Japan. I'm fifth generation."

"You know what the hell I mean. And you walked out six months before you were eligible for retirement—"

"I was tired of the Bureau."

"You could have stuck it out six more months!"

"And then I'd have missed the job I wanted. Nobody's going to run a police department without a chief for six months."

"A twenty-man police department. You could be doing so damn much better—"

"I'm doing what I want to do."

"How much are you making here?"

"That's none of your damn business."

"And you with a law degree—"

"Can we get on to why I'm supposed to be harboring a fugitive who's reportedly trying to kill me?"

"Because you're a stupid, quixotic son of a bitch."

"You're repeating yourself. That's no answer at all."

"You were accused of killing your wife. You didn't do it. So now you've decided nobody who's accused of killing his wife did it. Hansen was convicted of killing his wife. Ergo, in your book he's got to be innocent."

"That's the most idiotic excuse for reasoning I've ever heard in my life. I know just as well as you do that whenever somebody's murdered in a domestic setting you look first at the spouse. I don't know whether Hansen did it or not. I can tell you there was a lousy job of investigating done on the case. But that's all I know right now."

"So what are you doing, hiding Hansen while you try to reinvestigate a three-year-old murder?"

"I am not hiding Hansen. I have never seen Hansen in my life. In view of his having threatened to kill me, I am not exactly eager to see him. However, I can tell you that nothing you have said in here today would have persuaded me to relinquish him if I *did* happen to be hiding him."

"Damn it, Shigata—"

"Do you want to check my office? Do you want to check my jail cells? Do you want to check my storage rooms? My locker rooms? My house? My car? Or do you want to get the hell out of my office and leave me to do my work?"

Barlow's mood was not noticeably improved in the next thirty seconds, when a polite knock at the door was followed at once by Ted Barlow. "What the hell are you doing here?" Jim Barlow demanded.

"I work here. Chief, you want to initial this watch list?"

Shigata glanced over the watch list, nodded, and initialed it. "Why so early?"

"Because I thought you might want to go home early."

"Probably not, but good thinking." He slid the watch list back across the desk, and Ted Barlow departed, followed very closely by his father.

Shigata would have given a lot to hear that discussion. But all he heard of it was Ted Barlow's loud and angry reply: "Shove it. I don't work for you *or* the Bureau."

Jim Barlow slammed the door hard when he left, and Ted Barlow quite peacefully proceeded toward the locker room, leaving Shigata quivering with silent laughter.

Quinn, who had been an observer, commented, "It didn't take you long."

"What didn't take me long?"

"To start looking at the Bureau the way most city cops look at the Bureau."

"Right. It didn't take me long. Are you on duty right now?"

"No, why?"

"You live here?"

"Are you suggesting I go home?"

"The thought had crossed my mind."

"Actually, I've got to go to church," Quinn said.

Shigata looked up, startled. "Church?"

"Yeah. Church. You got any problem with that?"

48

"None at all. You just don't usually—"

"It's sort of this way. I go to church with Nguyen or Nguyen gets on my case. If you know what I mean. I'll be back up here right after noon."

"You're off today. Stay home and get some rest."

"Right. And leave you by yourself to cope with the FBI, the Rangers, locating that missing woman, protecting yourself—"

"I'm a big boy. I can brush my hair myself now. Stay home and get some rest."

"We'll see."

"Anyway, I don't have any Rangers to cope with."

"Guess again. H'lo, Truax. Bye, Truax." Quinn headed out the door.

"What was that all about?" Wesley Truax inquired, gazing at his retreating back.

"We're having a slight difference of opinion. I want him to get some rest, and he doesn't want to."

"That's a new one." Truax sat down. Nothing but the pistol at his hip and the circled star pinned to his gray chino shirt suggested he was one of the famous Texas Rangers; his boots were plain black leather, his hair was graying, and he was wearing metal-rimmed bifocals.

But Shigata had known him about as long as he'd lived in Texas.

"I guess you're here to yell at me about Hansen too."

"Actually, I wasn't going to yell. Why? Who's been yelling at you?"

"Barlow thinks I know where Hansen is and I'm hiding him."

"Barlow's an ass. Though hiding Hansen might not be such a bad idea."

"You know Hansen?"

"Oh, yeah, I've known him ten or twelve years."

"Good. What can you tell me about him?"

"Well, I wouldn't care to find out that he was hunting me," Truax said.

"What I want to know is, what's he hunting me for?"

49

Shigata demanded. "I mean, I've never so much as laid eyes on the guy."

"Danged if I know. Doesn't sound like Hansen to me, but Huntsville seems pretty sure about it."

"You think he was really guilty?"

Truax shrugged. "People do funny things. Tell me about this missing woman, this Shelley Morgan. What relation is she to him?"

"Sister-in-law. Ex-sister-in-law, I guess. I don't know. His wife's sister, anyway. She was raising Hansen's boy."

"And she went missing last night."

"Sometime yesterday. Reported last night."

"And the car turned up with blood in it."

"Yeah."

"How much blood?"

"Enough."

"You think she's dead, then?"

"I think she's dead. I think she died in that car and then somebody got the body out and stashed it somewhere."

"Why?"

"Why does anybody do anything?" Shigata asked. "You got any business here, or do you just want to sit and hassle me?"

"Touchy today, are we?"

"You'd be touchy too if somebody with an IQ of about a hundred and eighty-five was stalking you. Look, I've got a desk full of work."

"On Sunday."

"And every other day. I've got slots for twenty sworn people and six civilians. I have sixteen sworn officers and four civilians. Every time I get somebody half trained, they take off to where they can get more pay. I can't blame 'em for that. But it makes things a little hairy. Quinn and I are both working twelve hours, seven days."

"You can do that only so long."

"No shit."

"Okay, I'll get out of your hair. Call me if you need me."

Shigata waited until he heard the front door of the building

50

close. Then he sorted through the files on his desk. Personnel file, Steven Hansen. Personnel file, Dale Shipp. All personnel files, open and closed, were in a file cabinet in the chief's office. That made them easy for him to get ahold of.

Case file. The murder of Lillian Hansen and Gaylene Hansen. Case closed. Cleared by arrest.

With only one lab report, a letter from the state crime lab in Austin:

Slug #1 reportedly found beneath the body of victim #1 Lillian Hansen, slug #2 reportedly found beneath the head of vict. #2 Gaylene Hansen, slug #3 reportedly found beneath body of vict. #3, a cocker spaniel dog, were fired from the same revolver as slug #4, test slug collected by Chief Dale Shipp.

The report went on at some length discussing lands, grooves, and other identifying characteristics. No mention of the make of gun. Shipp hadn't asked that. The lab answers only what it is asked. There was no other useful information. No autopsy records. No record of fingerprint work. No fingerprints and palm prints of the deceased. Two or three half-assed reports. Nothing else except photographs. Excellent photographs. They looked as if they must have come from Galveston. Shigata didn't look yet at the DA's files, which would certainly be in better order. Before doing that, he wanted a look at the physical evidence.

When it came back from Galveston he'd stuffed it into the narcotics locker, actually a safe that served to hold evidentiary firearms, cash, and jewelry as well as narcotics.

The safe was located directly behind Shigata's desk chair.

Shigata turned around, opened the safe, and began methodically taking our all of its contents. He ought to have inventoried this as soon as he got it back, but he just hadn't had time, and it had seemed low priority.

Now it was high priority.

Three hours later he had most of the stuff back into the safe, and an inventory in pencil on a yellow legal pad on his desk. He'd kept one thing out.

51

One plastic evidence bag with the right case number on it. It contained a Dan Wesson .357 magnum service revolver.

Partially loaded, three shots fired. It hadn't been cleaned since those shots were fired.

A Dan Wesson. But those slugs . . . That was funny.

Shigata turned the bag over carefully, studying it from every angle.

The case number was written on it in ballpoint pen. Description of where it was found, the date, the time. Two sets of initials on it. "DS." That was Dale Shipp. "DB." Most likely that was Dan Buchanan. He'd died sixteen feet away from where Shigata was now sitting, a little over a year ago.

The bag had three staples in it. There were no other staple holes. Either the bag had never been unstapled after the first time it was stapled shut, or somebody had been very, very careful about restapling. Which wasn't likely.

So no test slug was ever fired from this gun. And that was interesting. Very damned interesting indeed.

Turning the clear plastic bag carefully, Shigata could still make out, faint but visible, the lines of fingerprints on the trigger and the backstrap. Fingerprints that had never been lifted.

That was funny too, because one thing the half-assed reports did mention was that there were no usable latents on the gun. Which meant Shipp was lying. Again.

Something else caught Shigata's attention and he carefully opened the bag. He dusted with mag powder, which isn't supposed to be usable on guns, but experience had taught him it worked best. He lifted prints, looked at them, looked at Hansen's fingerprint card that had been stuck in the bag of evidence. He emptied the revolver, looked at the loaded cartridges and the empties. Then he sat and thought.

Five minutes later, he whistled. "Son of a bitch!" he said softly.

He wished Quinn were there, because he wanted to talk with Quinn fast.

Well, it was twelve-fifteen. Quinn would be in soon. The

chances of his obeying orders and staying home this afternoon were exactly zero.

Hansen had heard a lot of yelling and door banging, somewhere in the building this morning. He'd slipped back into the storage room about nine-thirty Saturday night, bringing with him a couple of sandwiches, another quart of milk, and a couple of Cokes because he could drink them hot, but the milk wouldn't be fit to drink after it got hot. He'd slipped out sometime during the night, to use the mayor's restroom, but he was afraid to try to flush. He'd worked deep nights. As silent as the building gets then, an officer on duty could hear a toilet flush half a block away.

He'd waited. And waited. And waited.

Waited until he'd finished the milk and the sandwiches and the Coke. Waited until the banging and the yelling stopped. Even waited until he finished reading another couple of chapters of the the book he'd had in his pocket when he escaped, which happened to be *Pale Fire*.

And he went on waiting.

He'd told Todd the truth—he wasn't afraid to die. Not anymore. He'd been living with death at his shoulder so long that it didn't seem real anymore. They'd set his execution date twice already. He kept on appealing, not because he thought it would do any good but just from some dogged refusal to give up even if everybody else had given up on him. Even Amnesty International wasn't too interested in a man who'd shot his wife and daughter.

Only now that the time of his death was in his own hands rather than somebody else's, he was finding it easy to dawdle. He hadn't realized, yesterday, that he was suicidal. He realized it now. In killing Shipp, he'd planned—subconsciously—to also kill himself.

And now he realized he didn't really want to die. It wasn't that he was afraid, he wasn't afraid. It was just that he'd rather stay alive as long as there was one more book to read, one more puzzle to sort out, one more day to watch sea gulls on the beach.

But he wasn't going back to prison. Not even if he had to turn his pistol on himself as soon as he'd killed Dale Shipp.

The building was utterly silent now. Either Shipp was there or he wasn't. If he was, it would be over with —fast— one way or the other. If he wasn't—if he wasn't, Hansen would do his damnedest to get back into this storeroom unseen and try again tomorrow.

He drew the pistol. Emptied the cartridges out into his hand. Spun the cylinder. Looked at each cartridge individually, carefully. Spun the cylinder one more time. Reloaded. Six cartridges. Six soft-nosed lead cartridges he'd dum-dummed himself.

He went to the door that led into the police station. The locks had been changed, but the new lock yielded to his pocketknife blade as easily as the city hall lock had done, and he stepped, very quietly, into the building he'd worked in—and out of—for twenty years.

It looked just the same as it always had, and for a moment tears threatened to blind his eyes. But he dashed them back and walked, very quietly, setting each foot down flat where the boards didn't squeak. (Oh yes, he knew every squeaky board, every tile that didn't sit quite right, in this building.)

The muster room sat right outside the chief's office. He'd made it that far and hadn't seen anybody yet. And yes, there was somebody in the chief's office, somebody leaning over something on his desk, so engrossed in it he hadn't looked up at all.

Hansen eased forward. The door was open. Not much farther. Not much farther.

Then he was standing in the doorway to the chief's office, pointing his pistol down at a sleek dark head. *Son of a bitch has lost weight. And damned if I don't think he's started dyeing his hair.*

Fire now! Before he has time to look up!

No. I want him to know who. I want him to know why.

"Look at me, you son of a bitch."

The man looked up.

And it wasn't Dale Shipp.

54

$\triangledown$

Chapter 5

SHIGATA LOOKED DIRECTLY INTO the muzzle of the gun. With some difficulty, he forced his eyes up past it, just as the man behind the gun yelled, "Oh, shit!" and then demanded, "Who the hell are you?"

"Mark Shigata. You, I gather, are Steve Hansen?"

"Yeah." Hansen looked puzzled, but made no move to lower the gun.

"I hear you want to kill me." Shigata could see Quinn, pistol drawn, moving in behind Hansen, but Quinn wouldn't need any telling as to how dangerous this situation was. A bullet can outrun just about anything else, but it can't outrun another bullet.

"What would I want to kill you for?" Hansen asked blankly. "I don't even know you."

"I'm the chief of police in Bayport."

"But—" Hansen glanced down at the .38 as if he had never seen it before. "I don't even know you. I don't want to kill you. It's Shipp I want to kill."

"Well, if you don't want to kill me, would you mind putting that pistol down? The view of it from this end is not edifying. Or amusing."

"Oh. Yeah. Sorry." Hansen started to lower the gun, only to have it neatly removed from his hand. He glanced around. "Hi, Quinn."

55

"H'lo, Hansen. What are you doing with a son-of-a-bitchin' Colt?"

"I like a Colt."

"I wouldn't give two cents for one, not with that damn two-stage trigger. Uh, by the way, if you'd astarted to pull that trigger your ass would've been dog meat."

"My ass is dog meat anyway, or are you behind on the news?"

"Not near as behind as you are, coming after Shipp where he ain't been in years. What happened to all them newspapers you was s'posed to be getting?"

"I read them. They don't say much about Bayport. Too small, I guess."

"You ought to get the Bayport weekly."

"I tried," Hansen said. "They won't mail it."

"If I could get a word in," Shigata said politely, and waited for silence before adding, "Hansen, I'm not so sure your ass is necessarily dog meat."

"What's that supposed to mean?" Hansen focused his eyes on the top of Shigata's desk. Case files. Personnel files. A plastic evidence bag. Some fingerprint lifts, a handful of cartridges, a— "That's my pistol."

"Yes. That's your pistol. Sit down."

Hansen sat. "You've got guts," he observed.

"I've also got your pistol," Shigata answered. "At least one of them. And Al's got one. Is that all, or do we have to pat you down?"

"That's all," Hansen said, "but you can pat me down if you want to."

"Never mind," Shigata said. "You wouldn't be nearly that cooperative if you were holding. Is that book any good?"

"What book?" Hansen glanced down at his pocket, where *Pale Fire* was protruding. "That one. Yeah, I like it. You want it?"

"No, I want that pistol Al's holding . . . this one yours too, Hansen?'

"Yessir."

"How'd you get it back?"

56

"Nobody ever took it away from me."

"Where'd you have it stashed?"

"Fifth Amendment."

Shigata chuckled. "Okay. You win that round. How long have you had this one?"

"Fifteen years. Twelve, if you don't count the last three. I knew where it was, but I couldn't exactly lay hands on it."

"Right." Shigata flipped the cylinder out, emptied cartridges out into his hand. "What other handguns do you have?"

"This is it."

"What other handguns *did* you have?"

"This is it," Hansen repeated. "I used to have a .30-30 rifle and a twelve-gauge shotgun, but I sold them. And I never have owned any other handguns."

"Ever use anybody else's?"

"No," Hansen said. "Why are you asking me all this?"

"For now, say I'm nosy," Shigata turned a cartridge over, looked at it carefully. "You always cut an *X* in the nose of your slug?"

"Yes, sir."

"Why don't you just buy hollow nose?"

"I don't know. Habit, I guess."

"Could you tell the difference between yours and somebody else's?"

"I don't know. Probably."

Shigata leaned across the desk. "These both yours?"

"This one is." Hansen turned the other over, carefully. "No. This one isn't."

"You're right. It's mine. . . . All these yours?"

Hansen examined the three cartridges. "I think so."

"I think so too. You ever use copper jackets?"

"No."

"Was your wife right-handed?"

"Yes."

"And you're right-handed. Anybody in your family left-handed?"

"Yeah, both my kids. Gaylene and Todd. Why?"

"Who worked the crime scene at your house? Shipp?"

"Galveston."

"Shipp couldn't do a crime scene on a paper bag," Quinn inserted.

"They do a neutron activation on your hands?"

"Yes."

"A trace metal?"

"No. What good would that do? It was my pistol. I'd definitely had it in my hand within the last twelve hours."

"With your finger on the trigger?"

"I don't know. Probably. I do that."

"Did they do one on your wife?"

"One what? Neutron activation? I guess so. I didn't see it, but I know they did some kind of firearms residue. If you mean a trace metal, I don't know. I doubt Shipp knows about trace metal. He's stupid."

"Galveston isn't."

"That's true. What are you getting at?"

"If Galveston did the crime scene, I'm betting Galveston would do a neutron activation and a trace metal on your wife. But you know what? There's no report in here of any firearms residue test of any kind, or any trace metal test on anybody. Does that say anything to you?"

"Maybe," Hansen said. "I know what they said in court, anyway."

"What did they say in court?" Shigata asked, apparently casually.

"A lot of stuff."

"Was it true?"

"Some of it was. Not all. I didn't kill my wife and daughter."

"Suppose you tell me what the case was against you."

"You've got records on your desk. I can see them from here. Why don't you just read them?"

"Play like I can't read. Tell me what the case was against you."

Hansen shrugged. "You into playing games?"

"Say I am, anyway. You know how to play games, right?"

"Wrong," Hansen said. "They never let me learn when I was a kid. I was too busy being the boy genius."

58

"Happens. Now tell me about the case."

"All right, all right," Hansen said. "I guess I owe you that, anyway, after scaring you half to death. Okay, I—Let me start out by telling you what *did* happen. It was Friday. Middle of July and hotter'n hell. Lillian and I had an argument."

"What about?"

"Gaylene. There was something wrong with Gaylene, and Lillian wouldn't tell me what."

"Gaylene's the other victim? The girl?"

"Yeah," Hansen said. "Okay, so we had a quarrel, and I—" He related the evening, the morning. "So there was my .357 lying on the floor, and Lillian—" He shook his head. "Kipling wrote a poem about a killing, you know? Nobody else would describe a killing in a poem, but he did. There's one line, something like 'With a small blue mark on his forehead and the back blown out of his head.' I don't know where the hell he got the small blue mark, because a bullet hole's not small and blue, at least none I ever saw, but the rest of it's sure as hell the truth. My wife . . . had the back blown out of her head. Gaylene—Gaylene was shot in the back of the head. They didn't make me look at her face, and I'll always be thankful for that. But even so—" He shook his head for a moment before resuming, his voice not entirely steady. "Well—there weren't any fingerprints on the gun. Not to be of any use, anyway."

Shigata, who knew that wasn't true, didn't say so. He just said, "Go on."

"Shipp said he'd fired a test slug out of my pistol. Then he said he hadn't fired one because the barrel might be fouled, and so he just went out to where I'd been practicing and got a slug from there."

"And nobody else ever practiced there?"

"Nobody else who might have shot my wife."

"So Shipp switched his story."

"Yes. But he said he didn't. He said I'd just misunderstood him. What difference does it make? Shipp's a liar. Everybody knows that but the DA and the jury."

59

"Shipp wouldn't know the truth if it bit him," Quinn confirmed. "Boss, I told you that."

"So you did," Shigata agreed. "Was that all, Hansen? Seems like damned little to convict a man."

"There was more." Hansen told about the dog, about the psychiatrists' testimony.

"But it was all circumstantial?" Shigata asked. "Nobody could prove you fired the gun?"

"No. But then, murder convictions are usually circumstantial. You know that. And everybody knew it was my gun."

"I don't see any evidence that it was your gun."

"You didn't see the lab report?"

"I saw the lab report. It didn't mention a gun."

"It didn't need to mention a gun," Hansen said. "Just that the bullets matched—"

"The bullets matched each other," Shigata interrupted. "That doesn't prove they matched the gun. That's why the lab always wants to have the gun there, not just a test slug, before they run comparisons. But Shipp didn't send it in."

Hansen shrugged. "So? You've got three slugs and you've got a gun fired three times. What more do you want?"

"I want a lot more," Shigata said. "Now, let me ask you something else. If you had the choice—which you don't, because I'm not going to let you kill Dale Shipp—but if you had the choice, which would you rather do, kill Shipp and go right back where you were or start pushing up daisies, or get your son back and get your job back and put Shipp where you were?"

Hansen sat straight up, unbelieving joy blazing across his face. But then he slumped back into the chair. "What do you think you are, the miracle man?"

"Let's say I'm not Dale Shipp. Al, you with me? Or do you want to go home and not know anything? We could be risking prison ourselves before it's over."

Quinn shut the office door and sat down. "Hansen, if I find out you're lying to us, you won't make it back to Huntsville. I'll burn you myself."

60

"The best thing I can do for you," Shigata said, "is send you back to prison while I work on this myself."

Without any apparent haste to tip anybody off, but far too quickly for either Quinn or Shigata to stop him, Hansen took Quinn's pistol and returned to his chair, with the muzzle under his own chin, pointed in such a direction that if the gun were fired it would take out most of his brain. "I'm not going," he said in a perfectly reasonable, conversational tone. "I've been there for three years. I'm not going to hurt either one of you. I have no reason to. But I can't be hurt any worse than I've already been hurt. I'm not going back to prison."

"What about Todd?"

"What about him? Every time they set an execution date, the news vultures go camp on his front steps. You think I don't know that? At least this'll be the last time. It'll be over for him too."

"He believes you're innocent."

"That's not what he told me."

"It's damn sure what he told me. Who do you plan on him living with, now that Shelley's dead?"

"What are you talking about? Shelley's not dead. I saw her yesterday."

"Where? When?"

"Two blocks from her house. Almost noon. She was driving a green car—Cougar, I think."

"She see you?"

"No." Hansen was beginning to relax, though not enough yet for either Quinn or Shigata to feel like going for the pistol. "If she'd seen me, you'd have known about it within the next thirty seconds."

"Todd reported her missing last night about midnight. He said she never got home when he was expecting her at noon. We found her car this morning with a lot of blood in it."

"She couldn't have not gotten home. She wasn't two blocks from her house. Todd was waiting for her. Todd . . ." His voice trailed off into silence as he rethought the case. Then the color began to drain from his face. He said, "No—no—" and the muscles in his throat worked and his

61

finger began to tighten on the trigger.

Shigata and Quinn both dived for the pistol, which went off once during the melee. Then Hansen was disarmed and back on the chair, sobbing, sobbing—

The dispatcher at the door, face white. "What's happening—"

Shigata rounded on her furiously. "Get back to your post. Everything's under control in here." He glanced, with some annoyance, at the wood paneling behind his head, now sporting a freshly splintered hole.

Hansen went on sobbing. Until finally he lifted his head and said hoarsely, "Why'd you stop me? Who gave you the right to make me go on living when I'm through living?"

"The state of Texas," Shigata said. "Now, would you mind telling me what this is all about?"

Hansen gestured widely with one hand. "It's just over, that's all. It's over with. You don't have an investigation. It's over. Forget it."

"You're telling me you killed your wife?"

"Yeah. I did it before I went to the beach."

"And you're telling me you killed your daughter."

"Stepdaughter. Yeah. Her too."

"And Shelley."

"Yeah. Shelley. I—uh—got her to stop the car, and—"

"Where'd you leave the car?"

"I forget."

"Where'd you put the body?"

"I don't remember. You'll find it eventually. Go outside and look for where the buzzards circle. They'll lead you right to it."

"You're a pretty lousy liar, you know it?" Shigata asked conversationally.

"Not enough experience," Hansen muttered.

"And I guess we better get you to sign a Miranda—"

"I'll sign anything you want me to sign. I'll sign a confession. After I do it, just give me back the pistol for about two seconds. That's all it'll take. You can say it was an accident."

"He didn't do it, you know," Shigata said.

"Who didn't do what?"

"Todd. He didn't kill his aunt. Or his mother and sister."

"I never said he did."

"Right," Shigata said dryly. "I noticed that. But I watched you thinking. You know your wife and daughter were killed with copper jackets?"

"Yes. I told the jury I never used copper jackets. The prosecutor said that was all the more reason why I would use copper jackets to commit murder, because I never used them any other time. Or else I might have absentmindedly reloaded from somebody else's box, at the police station. And he was right. I might've. I never did before, but I might've. Give me back my pistol. I won't shoot myself now."

"Which one?"

"The Colt. The little one. I can't get the other in a shoulder holster."

"What do you want it for? I already told you I won't let you kill Shipp. If you don't want to kill yourself, what do you want it for?"

"Because I want it. I just want it, that's all."

"That's no reason why I should give it to you. You've had twenty years of law-enforcement experience. Out of all that, can you come up with one reason why I should hand a pistol over to an escapee from Death Row?"

"Because it's mine?" Shigata didn't answer. "In case I need it?"

"For what?"

"I don't know. Just in case. You're not going to do it, are you?"

"Would you, if you were in my shoes?"

"I wish you had some idea how I feel," Hansen said bitterly.

"I have a far better idea than you might think," Shigata answered. "Now what? Do we talk like sane normal human beings, or do I slap handcuffs on you and call Huntsville to come get you?"

Hansen covered his face with his hands just as the door opened and Claire Barndt came in. She stopped short. "Oh, I'm sorry, I didn't mean to interrupt—"

63

"Some of us knock on closed doors," Shigata told her as Hansen dropped his hands back to his knees, his eyes visibly widening as he looked at her.

"I'm sorry, she repeated. "I didn't mean to— Is something wrong?" she asked Hansen. "You look—"

"No. I'm all right. I'm—all right now," Hansen said, still looking at her.

"Barndt, you're not on duty now, are you?" Quinn asked.

"No, sir, but I didn't know if either of you would be here tonight, and the dispatch kind of got on my case last night because I didn't have the watch bill initialed. So—"

"So that's why Barlow was in here this morning," Shigata said. "You will kindly tell dispatch— Never mind, *I'll* tell dispatch. You and Barlow initial your own watch bills. That's a watch commander's responsibility. Among other things."

"Yes, sir."

Hansen watched her leave. Then he asked, "Are you making watch commanders out of children now?"

"She's twenty-six," Quinn said shortly.

Hansen took a deep breath. "Thanks for not telling her who I am, and thanks for stopping me. I guess. I hope. Even if you had proof on your desk at this moment that I'm innocent—and I don't for a second believe you do—I'd still have to go back to Huntsville long enough to get the paperwork sorted out, and that could take years. Thing is, I don't want to walk at my son's expense. No, I don't think he killed his mother and sister. But—he was on pot at the time."

"That doesn't usually lead to violence," Shigata pointed out.

"I know that. But what I don't know is whether he was on anything else. And I don't know whether he's on anything now."

"You saw him yesterday."

"For half an hour, for the first time in three years. That's not enough to tell anything."

"Hansen," Shigata said, "you insist you're not guilty. You don't seem to think Todd is. So who do *you* think killed your wife and daughter?"

"I honestly think she did it herself. Lillian, I mean."

"Why?" Quinn asked very quietly.

A long silence. Then Hansen said, "I don't want to answer that."

"If you want us to help you, you're going to have to give us what you've got," Shigata told him.

"Then just call Huntsville. Because I won't tell you."

Shigata picked up the telephone handset. Hansen watched him silently. Shigata slammed it back down. "Damn it, man, I'm not going to let you do this!"

"Why?" Hansen inquired. "You don't owe me anything. You don't even know me. The investigation's over. I've already been convicted and sentenced. I walked in here and pointed a gun at your head and damn near pulled the trigger. Just call Huntsville. You can't play a ball that's not in your court."

"No, but I can damn well start a new game!" Shigata returned. "Hansen, I don't know for sure you're innocent. But I damn well know there's too much wrong with this case for me to call you guilty. Right now I want to rework this case. And that means asking you questions."

"Why?" Hansen asked.

"Look, you stupid son of a bitch," Quinn growled, "we're making watch commanders out of children—Barlow's just twenty-two—because we don't have anybody but Shigata and me with experience. We're both working twelve hours, seven days. You're sitting there with twenty years of experience, and you've spent three years doing nothing but sit on your ass. Now, damn it, you can quit arguing and get back to work. Me and Shigata are trying to think, and you're being nothing but trouble. The least you can do is start answering questions."

Hansen began to laugh, very quietly. And then he said, "All right. Ask your questions."

"I want you to start with this one," Shigata said. "Where did Lillian get the copper-jacketed shells?"

Dead silence.

"I asked a question," Shigata said. "Did you hear it?"

"I don't know," Hansen said.

"You don't know if you heard it?"

"Stop it. You don't have to do this to me. I said I'd answer you."

"I heard you've got an IQ of about a hundred and eighty-five."

"You heard wrong. It's about a hundred and forty-five. Or was. It's probably shrunk."

"I'm inclined to think it has," Shigata said. "Because it looks to me like you've been doing a hell of a lot of fuzzy thinking Now, where did Lillian get the copper-jacketed shells?"

"I don't know," Hansen said. "I've wondered that all along, and I never have come up with an idea that made sense. I have never bought copper-jacketed shells in my life. Not for me, anyway. I don't like them. I don't even know why anybody makes them. I want soft-lead hollow-nose, and yes, I know dum-dums are against the Geneva Convention, but I'm not a soldier. I'm—I was a cop."

"Would Lillian walk into a store and buy them?"

"Lillian wouldn't know—wouldn't have known how to buy ammo. I don't think she even knew how to load a pistol. I wanted to teach her how to shoot, and she wouldn't try."

"Then why was it so easy for you to believe she'd shoot her daughter and herself?" Shigata asked.

"It wasn't. It wasn't. It never was. Look, I've spent three years trying to make sense of it. It was just—I couldn't think of any other answer. And I still can't."

"If you think Lillian killed herself, then why did you want to kill Shipp?" Shigata was asking questions fast, deliberately trying not to give Hansen time to think up answers, and the pressure was working. In the small, close room, Hansen was sweating. "You're blaming Shipp for what Lillian did," Shigata pointed out. "Or at least for what you think Lillian did. You're an intelligent man. I think you're a fair man. So why do you blame Shipp?"

Hansen took a long, deep breath. "What I have to say doesn't go outside this room unless it absolutely has to."

"Agreed," Shigata said.

"Gaylene was my stepdaughter. Here's the background. Lillian—got pregnant. Her senior year in high school. Shipp was the father. They got married just long enough to give the baby a name. I think he raped her, but I'm not sure. She didn't want to talk about it. I tried to press her once, and she started crying and I didn't ask again. Okay. They were divorced by the time Gaylene was six months old. I was already on the police department by then. Patrolman. Shipp was sergeant. She—Lillian—was trying to work at a Dairy Queen and support herself and the baby. Her parents had thrown her out. I don't know if Shipp was paying any child support. If he was, it wasn't much. I—she looked pretty valiant to me. She tried so hard—she tried so hard—and I had—I wasn't making much. Quinn, you know what it was like, you wouldn't work for the police department then because the pay was so shitty, but I figured nothing could be worse for her than it already was. I married her. Shipp thought it was funny. Then, he thought it was funny. I was taking his cast offs. Me, the whiz kid, the college-boy cop, I was taking his leftovers. But I didn't care what he thought. I didn't marry Lillian because I loved her, I married her because I respected her and and I was sorry for her, but I did love her. Later. I did love her. I don't think she ever quite believed that, because she knew I'd married her because I was sorry for her, and it was always like—like she didn't think she had the right to be loved. But I did. I did. And we had Todd a couple of years later and then she had three miscarriages, and the doctor said there wasn't any use trying again because she was Rh negative and the babies were all Rh positive and she was sensitized against their blood—it was like an allergy in her. So that was that, and I got my wings clipped. You know what I mean."

"A vasectomy?"

"Yeah. It was the easiest thing to do. Only she felt real bad about that. I think she somehow got it into her head it was like castration and she thought she'd done something terrible to me, and I never could convince her I was okay, I didn't lose anything I needed. She was always going around feeling guilty about things. If she burned the green beans, she felt guilty. If I left a ballpoint pen in my shirt and she washed it, she felt guilty. If the electric bill went up five bucks, she felt guilty. If a late frost like we had this week nipped the garden, she felt guilty. Like there was anything she could do about it. Understand?"

"Yeah," Shigata said. "Go on."

"Okay. Shipp—wasn't interested in Gaylene. I didn't care. He didn't have to be. I was Daddy. She didn't need two Daddys. It was tough sometimes, financially I mean, but you know, we were making it okay, and if he got his jollies out of ribbing me, so what, it wasn't hurting me any." He took a breath. "That's how it was. Until Gaylene was thirteen. And all of a sudden she didn't look like a kid anymore. She went, like it was overnight, she went from being a kid to— Quinn, you saw her."

"Yes. I saw her."

"The face that launched a thousand ships and burnt the topless towers of—" He paused, took a deep breath. "She was all beauty, all mystery. Like Helen and Cleopatra and Salome and Lygeia all rolled into one. But she was also a teenage kid who threw her clothes on the floor and bitched about homework and dishwashing. I saw that. I don't think Shipp did. It was like—you were on a jungle path and you saw a perfect orchid. Could you see it and take a picture of it and leave it to grow? Or would you have to yank it up by the roots and crush it to make it yours? I could leave it to grow. Shipp couldn't. We used to wonder, Lillian and I, where she'd gotten it from. The black hair and brown eyes, those were from Shipp, of course; Lillian was a blue-eyed blond like me, but for the rest of it—God only knows. Shipp's not much to look at, and Lillian, time she was thirty she looked like a fat little German *hausfrau*. I used to kid her—her face was so round and rosy, and she'd braid that taffy-colored hair and pin the braids up on the top of her head. I used to call her the apple dumpling gang. I—*I'm sorry*—"

The last two words came from between clenched teeth.

He was crying again. But there was no incipient hysteria this time, only honest grief, and Shigata and Quinn simply waited.

"I don't want to think she did it," Hansen said finally. "But I just don't see any other answer. Because Todd—"

"Todd what?" Shigata asked when Hansen paused.

"Yesterday Todd told me she—Gaylene—was pregnant and asked me if I— well. And he was scared of me when I first walked in. He was afraid. If he'd— I don't even want to say this. But if Todd—he wouldn't have had any reason. Not any reason at all. I know I'm incoherent. He wouldn't have had any reason to kill them unless he was the father. He was thirteen. It wasn't biologically impossible, I suppose. But in human terms—no. He wouldn't have asked me if I was the father if he was the father. And he wouldn't have been afraid of me unless he thought he had some reason to be. Todd thought I did it. He wouldn't have thought I did it if he did it."

"Unless he blanked it out," Quinn said. "There was this movie I saw on TV, Stella Stevens was playing an ax murderer, and— Never mind. Forget I said it."

"Why would Todd have thought you could be the father?" Shigata asked.

"Because I was an adult male living in the same house with her," Hansen said flatly.

"You never saw her, Shigata," Quinn said. "Believe me. If you were male and alive, if you saw her once you'd never forget her."

"And I felt it," Hansen said. "Yes, of course I felt it. You couldn't be a man and not feel it. But you can look at an orchid and see that it's an orchid and not have to have it for yourself. She was my daughter. She wasn't my wife. She wasn't my property. Understand? But—Shipp didn't see it that way. He hadn't wanted a thing to do with her. And all of a sudden he did. And we couldn't stop it. I hadn't legally adopted her. I didn't think I needed to. Shipp wasn't interested. And then when he was interested he could have blocked the adoption. Do you understand what I'm saying? Do I have to spell it out?"

69

"I understand," Shigata said, "but I think you better spell it out anyway."

"There wasn't an autopsy," Hansen said. "There wasn't an autopsy because the investigating officer—Shipp—didn't want one and managed to convince the coroner it wasn't necessary. I don't know how he did it. I don't even think it was legal. I could have fought it, but I didn't. Shipp didn't want it, but I didn't either."

"You're saying Gaylene was pregnant by her father," Shigata said.

"I can't prove it. But she was. And with Lillian the way she was—always feeling guilty about everything—which would be easier? To face me with that? Or go put her and Gaylene beyond my reach forever?"

"Would you have been angry?"

"At whom?" Hansen asked. "At Shipp, yes. I'd have made him pay for it, one way or another. But not at Lillian. Not at Gaylene."

"But you never thought about Shipp? As a possible killer, I mean? Instead of Lillian?" Shigata asked.

"I thought about him a lot," Hansen admitted. "But I saw him that morning. He was as bad in shock as I was. And he was hating me. He'd mocked me before, but he hadn't hated me. And—I think he did love her. Gaylene, I mean. In a cockeyed bass-ackwards way, a twisted perverted way, but he did love her."

"And your only defense was that you were sleeping on the beach when it happened. None of this about Gaylene came out at the trial?" Shigata asked.

Hansen shook his head. "That she was Shipp's daughter. Nothing else. I—it wouldn't have done me any good, they'd just have said the baby was mine and there was no use dragging her name through the gutter."

"You ever hear of blood tests?" Quinn interrupted.

"What good would that do? I used to run the department blood drive every year. Shipp's type O positive. So am I. If it was happening now, there are genetic tests that can pinpoint paternity almost a hundred percent sure. But there weren't

70

three years ago. Or at least if there were, I didn't know it."

"An exhumation—" Quinn began, and stopped abruptly, at the almost identical expressions on Hansen's and Shigata's faces. "No?"

"No." Shigata said. "Not in a hot wet climate like this, three years later. No. Definitely not. No coffin, no embalming, is that good."

"Anyway," Hansen said, "there's more. I didn't tell you this. Shipp told me if I walked, he'd put it on Todd."

"Could he?" Shigata asked.

"I don't know," Hansen said. "Maybe he could. Especially with that cockamamie story about Todd sleeping through it all. He'd slipped out. But the way Shipp lies, you never really know where you are. Or aren't. I don't think he could. But I don't know for sure. And I won't walk at my son's expense."

Shigata looked down again at the papers, the files, the evidence on his desk. "Okay," he said, "we're going to work this case all over again. Or maybe I should just say we're going to work it, because it doesn't look to me as if it was ever worked before. Now, I'll say this again. I'm not sure you're innocent. But I am sure you shouldn't have been convicted. Shipp manipulated the hell out of the evidence even to get an indictment, much less a conviction. So I'm giving you the same benefit of the doubt I'd give any other suspect. See, one thing you may not understand, Hansen, because it's a situation you may not be used to. And that is, I'm just as smart as you are, and I have training you don't have. I'm going to be testing you in ways you'll never spot, until you do—or don't—trip yourself up. But I'm sticking my neck out doing it. Cross me and you'll wish you hadn't. Now, are you going to help me or get in my way?"

"If you want to send me back to Huntsville, go ahead. I've made about as much trouble here as I need to."

"I don't want to send you back to Huntsville. I need you here. Am I to take it that you've called off your hunting trip? Or should I say vendetta?"

A shrug. "I guess. You've got my pistol anyway."

"If I gave it back to you, what would you do with it?"

"Chief Shigata, I've never killed anything larger than a housefly in my life. I don't even hunt or fish. It's just as well I didn't find Shipp. I probably couldn't have done it anyway, unless he was shooting at me."

"What became of your uniforms when you were arrested?"

"Buchanan took them. I guess he turned them in. He certainly couldn't wear them."

"He turned them in," Quinn said. "I know where they are. Shigata, are you about to do what I think you're about to do? Because if you are, you're some more kind of crazy."

"Is there anybody in the department other than you and me who knows him?" Shigata asked.

"No, but Truax does, and I think Barlow does."

"Jim Barlow?" Hansen asked. "Yeah, he knows me. Doesn't like me much. I—uh—" A half-grin flashed across his face, and he wiped it away with his left hand. "He doesn't like me much."

"Then lay low while Truax and Barlow are around." Shigata wasn't in a mood to be amused.

"Shigata, I've policed here twenty years. Three quarters of the *town* knows me."

"I'm not sending you out to write traffic tickets," Shigata retorted. "Quinn, find him a uniform and then take a hike. You don't know anything about this."

"Like hell I don't. I hope you've given some thought to how they're gonna run this town without a police department. Come on, Hansen. We're *all* gonna be dog meat, but he's the boss."

At the door, Quinn glanced back at Shigata. *You're up to something*, he thought. *I'll back you, but I sure as hell wish I knew what you were doing.*

Shigata was hanging up the phone when Quinn and Hansen returned, Hansen in a sergeant's uniform that hung a little loosely on him, a black basketweave gunbelt, and no badge. "Here," Shigata said, and handed him a sergeant's badge.

Hansen looked at the number on it. "This is mine," he

said. "I mean *mine* mine. I bought it myself. How did you get it?"

"It came with the desk. We're about to roll. We've got a report of a body in a field. White female, late thirties. Bryce is on his way over there to check it out, but it's going to be Shelley Morgan. It's about two blocks from where her car turned up." He gestured toward the top of his desk. "I'd hoped we'd have time to get through this before we had to do anything else, but—"

He looked at Hansen's hard-set face. "Will this be too much for you to handle?"

"No. I never did like Shelley much. I'm sorry she's dead, but I can handle it. I'm just—worried about Todd."

"Keep that cap pulled as low as you can. What's wrong with your gunbelt? You can't go out with an empty holster."

"I don't have a hip holster for the Colt. It'd just fall out of this one."

"Then carry the .357. That's what the holster belongs to, isn't it?"

"Shigata, that's the gun my wife was killed with."

"You're sure about that?" Shigata asked. There was something in his voice that told Quinn what Shigata was up to. For some reason Quinn couldn't fathom, Shigata wanted to see how Hansen would react to a chance to carry that pistol.

"Hell, yes, I'm sure," Hansen said harshly. "I told you I saw it—" His voice broke for a moment and then steadied. "If you think I can just pick up the gun my wife was killed with and carry it like it was—like it was a baseball glove or something, man, you're crazy. I can't—"

"Your wife wasn't killed with that gun," Shigata interrupted.

"What are you talking about? I told you I saw—"

"You saw a gun lying in the middle of your living-room floor at your wife's feet. That doesn't mean it was the gun your wife was killed with. It wasn't. And that, my friend, I can prove."

Hansen eyed him for a moment. Then he took the .357 from the desk, snapped the cylinder open, and reached for the loose cartridges. Then he paused. "Shigata, the gun was fired," he said. "I know that. Shipp showed it to me. I left it fully loaded that night, and by morning there were three rounds fired out of it. So who—"

"I don't know," Shigata said. "That's one of the things we're going to have to find out. But I swear to you, this pistol did not kill your wife."

Hansen reached again for the cartridges.

"No," Shigata said quickly, "use these."

"These are copper jackets," Hansen objected.

"I know," Shigata said. "Use them anyway."

"Where'd you get them?"

"They came with the desk," Shigata said. "Ponder on that for a while, Hansen. Ponder on that."

He stopped again at the door. "Hansen," he said, "take the book out of your pocket. It doesn't go with the uniform."

Chapter 6

$\mathbf{A}$T THE OUTSIDE DOOR, Shigata paused. "Hansen, I didn't ask you if you want to do this. You don't have to. You can wait—"

"I want to," Hansen interrupted. "Believe me. I want to. No matter what happens next, I feel like a human being for the first time in over three years. I appreciate the chance you're taking—"

"The only real chance I'm taking is that you'll be recognized. I'm ready now to gamble that you're no killer."

"What changed your mind?"

"That's my business. Come on, there's a body waiting for us."

The body was of a slender white female, about five-four, 115 pounds, wearing navy-blue skirt, white blouse, navy-blue jacket. Late thirties. Dark brown hair neatly arranged. Blue eyes, brown plastic-framed glasses. Stockings, no shoes. Gold wristwatch, no rings. Neat manicure with clear fingernail polish. She was lying on her back, top of head pointing to the northeast, legs parallel, arms slightly out to sides, clothing disarranged as if she'd been dragged. She'd been shot once, right through the head.

In the sun that melted away the ice, the blood was still glisteningly fresh.

Shigata hadn't looked closely enough yet to determine which was the entry wound and which was the exit. Right now he was taking pictures.

"Yes, it's Shelley," Hansen said. "Not that there was any question about it."

"You can't formally identify the body," Shigata pointed out. "You aren't here."

"Then who— Not Todd. No way. I'd rather—"

"Hansen," Shigata said, "would you stop trying to commit suicide? Just stop it? It's getting very tiresome. What other relatives are there?"

"A sister in Tyler. Marion Morrison." He spelled the name. "I don't remember her address, but it'll be in Shelley's address book. Shigata, what I don't see is *why*. I don't know of any reason at all for anybody to kill Shelley."

"You said you didn't like her. Could be somebody else didn't like her."

"I didn't like her, but I certainly didn't dislike her to this extent. And I don't know why anybody else would. Not enough to kill her. She had—she had an off-and-on personality. But she could put on a show for outsiders. Most people liked her well enough. She could cut with her tongue, but she aimed it mostly at me. Hell hath no fury like—" He stopped.

"You're saying she wouldn't have minded if you'd decided to cheat on her sister," Shigata said delicately.

"She wouldn't have minded, no. Not if she was the—uh—beneficiary. She lied at the trial," Hansen added.

"Lied how?" Quinn asked.

"Said she saw me hit Lillian. And she never did. I never hit Lillian. Shipp might've, when she—Lillian—was married to Shipp, but I certainly didn't. I just don't go around hitting people."

"So you were pretty angry," Shigata said.

"Of course I was angry. I yelled at her while she was on the stand, and the judge threatened to have me either gagged or barred from the courtroom."

"Then everybody knew you were angry."

"Yes. But I probably would have been convicted anyway. She

didn't do it by herself. It takes too much energy to hate. I don't have enough to go around. I've been saving it all for Shipp."

"You could be lying," Quinn observed in a perfectly conversational tone.

Hansen turned to look at him. "Yes," he said, "I could be lying. I could be lying about all of it. Do I have reason to hate Shelley? Yes. She lied about me during the trial, she's been unkind to my son, she's done her dead-level best to turn my son against me—yes, I have sufficient motive. If that's what you think of as a motive. We all know murder's been done for less than that."

"A five-dollar loan, a shove in the dark—" Quinn said under his breath.

"Or just a misunderstood word," Hansen agreed. "Did I have a motive? Yes. Did I have opportunity? Yes. From the way this body looks, she must have died within half an hour or so after I saw her. Of course, I could renege on that, but there's always Todd to say what time I left the house. Did I have a weapon? We all know I had a weapon. Did I kill her? No. I did not. But I can't prove it. If you want to get me on this, you can. Real easy. Mark it cleared and the hell with whoever really did it. I've been through that once already."

"Hansen," Shigata said, "shut up for a minute or two, would you? Martyrs get tiring. You don't know Quinn very well. You know me even less. We've both been through some hells of our own. I can't say I'm sure you're innocent, because frankly I'm not. But I'm about ninety-nine percent sure, and that's good enough odds to gamble on. And I can't, in all honesty, tell you nobody wants to railroad you. I think somebody does. But it's neither of us. So knock it off."

"I'll tell you what we do have," said Quinn, who had squatted beside the body. "We have a damned smart murderer. Where was she shot?"

"In the car," Shigata said. "Sitting up in the car. Then he—whoever he was—shoved her over, drove the car over here, dumped her out, and then moved the car again."

"So where's the slug?" Quinn asked.

"It's not in the body, that's for sure," Shigata said.

"Clean through," Quinn agreed. "Entry hole on the right side of her head, exit on the left. The slug is not in the head. Hansen, did she have the car windows open?"

"She did when I saw her. I wondered why, as cold as it was."

"The windows were open when the car was found," Shigata said.

"So the slug went through her head and out the other window," Quinn said. "So we have no slug."

"So it doesn't do any good for me to offer my pistol for a test firing," Hansen said bitterly.

"I'm not sure about that," Shigata said. "If you two would move aside, I'd like to finish taking these pictures—"

A moment later he said, "We're assuming she was shot elsewhere and driven here. What if she was shot here?"

"What would she be doing here?" Hansen asked. "It's a good three miles from her house, and she was on her way there when I saw her."

"So she saw somebody else—" Quinn began.

Shigata interrupted. "Entry on the right, exit on the left. She was shot by a passenger. Who would she have as a passenger?"

"Todd," Hansen said in a totally passionless voice.

"Who else?" Shigata asked.

Hansen shook his head. "I don't know."

"When you saw her, you were walking away from her house and she was driving toward it. Which side of the road were you walking on?"

"I was facing oncoming traffic," Hansen said. "Means I saw the passenger's side better than I saw the driver's side. She didn't have a passenger then. If she'd had one, I would have seen it."

"So she picked up a passenger within two blocks," Shigata said, "or she did get home."

"I'm not going to shaft my son," Hansen said. "I already told you that."

"You're not shafting your son," Quinn said. "Does he have access to a pistol?"

"Not that I know of."

"How many guns did you have at home before any of this happened?" Shigata asked.

"I already told you that too."

"Tell me again."

"Two. One I'm wearing and the other is on your desk. I had a rifle and a shotgun, but you mean handguns. Anyway, I sold them."

"Did Shelley own a pistol? Or would you know?"

"I'd know. She didn't. Unless she's bought it within the last four years. Shigata, you're playing a concealed hand."

"I'm playing a concealed hand," Shigata confirmed. "For now. I've got some ideas I haven't had time to tell you about. Hansen, don't worry about your son. Honestly . . . Oh, shit, oh shit."

"What?" said Quinn, turning in the direction Shigata was looking, and then he too said, "Oh shit. Hansen, keep your head turned away. It's Truax."

"I think she was shot on the side of the road somewhere right along here," Shigata said quickly. "I'll tell you later why I think that. Right now, I want the two of you to start searching the field. There'll be a blowout from the side of her head—blood and tissue and stuff—not too far from where the car was parked. The slug'll have gone a lot farther, but that'll give us the starting point and maybe the trajectory. Hansen, don't look back this way until I've got rid of Truax."

"Right," Hansen said. He and Quinn walked away from the body, fanning apart, and Shigata turned to greet Truax.

"Didn't know you had a sergeant besides Quinn," Truax said, glancing at the two men, one in uniform and one in khaki work clothes, moving through the field in a methodical search pattern.

"I didn't. But Quinn went up to captain this week. This fellow has a lot of experience, and we're trying him out. Wes, you know I can't promote anybody I've got now. None of 'em have any experience at all—Barndt has the most, and that's just two years. I'll be raising her to corporal shortly, but she's not ready to be sergeant."

"You're a lot more talkative than you were this morning," Truax observed.

"Yeah, I had breakfast." He hadn't. But the explanation was as good as any.

"So this is Shelley Morgan?"

"So it would seem."

"Somebody sure as hell didn't like her. Well, damn it, I guess Hansen really did do it. Up to now I thought he'd been set up."

"How do you figure this says anything about Hansen?" Shigata asked.

"Who else would have reason to blow her away? And she was lying in her teeth at his trial, damn near as bad as Shipp was. Everybody but the jury could see that. Like I said, I figured then somebody'd put him in a trick, but now—"

"Suppose you wanted to kill Shelley Morgan for a private reason and didn't want anybody to suspect you," Shigata interrupted. "What better time could you have than this? Hansen's around. Blame it on him."

"But you couldn't count on Hansen breaking out," Truax objected.

"Right. So this would have to be spur of the moment," Shigata agreed. "But if you were hunting a good way to get rid of her—"

"Um. Yeah. See what you mean," Truax muttered. "But why would anybody else want to kill her?"

"That's what we're—what I'm going to have to find out."

From the far end of the field came a sudden shout. "Hey, Quinn! Over here!"

Shigata turned. Hansen, quite obediently, was facing away from Truax. But he was standing straight, holding one hand in the air. Quinn was headed toward him.

Truax didn't need a face. A remembered voice was enough. He shot a look of total wrath at Shigata and began to stride toward Hansen. Shigata caught hold of his arm. Truax jerked loose. "Get your hand off me, you lying son of a bitch!"

"It's my responsibility. I took it. He's in my custody. And

I wasn't lying to you this morning. I didn't get him until later."

"The hell he's in your custody. He's packing iron and you *let him*—"

"Wes, I'm telling you—"

"Hansen!" Truax shouted, at a distance of sixty feet.

Hansen spun, and his whole body seemed to sag. Truax went for his gun. Hansen didn't. He simply put his hands on top of his head.

"Wesley Truax, will you listen to me?" Shigata yelled. By now they were approaching Hansen and Quinn.

"You lying son of a bitch, I ought to arrest you too."

"If you want him, you'll have to take me with him. I said this is my responsibility—"

"Leave him alone, Wesley," Hansen said. "Quinn too. They're good men."

"You lying son of a bitch," Truax said for the third time. "You told me you hadn't seen—"

"I told you that before I saw him," Shigata said. "And I'm getting tired of being called a lying son of a bitch. I didn't lie to you. I just didn't tell you the whole truth."

"Wesley, it was after twelve when I walked into his office," Hansen said. "I walked in there with my pistol drawn and pointed at his head. I've been with him or Quinn ever since. So if you saw him earlier today, you saw him before he saw me."

"And three hours later he's got you walking around in a sergeant's uniform," Truax said. "Right. Hansen, will you get your hands down off the top of your head?"

"Then where would you like me to put my hands?"

"I don't care. Put 'em in your pockets. Stand on 'em if you want to, I don't give a shit. All I want to know is—"

"Truax, shut your mouth and open your ears," Shigata yelled. "I've got something I want to say to you. I'm about ninety-nine and ninety-nine one-hundredths percent sure this man did not commit murder. I believe he was set up, and I believe I know who did it and how he did it. Now, I want to tell you something that I know you don't want to hear, but I'm saying it anyway. I know something about what it does to innocent people to be imprisoned. I was born in prison. You probably didn't know that. But I was. Actually it wasn't prison, it was a concentration camp. My father and my mother and my uncles and my aunts and my grandparents and a whole lot more of my people were arrested and imprisoned. Why? For nothing. Not one single Japanese-American was ever convicted of one single act of espionage or sabotage during, before, or after World War Two. All the same, a lot of American citizens—many of them like us, third- and fourth- and fifth-generation Americans, with no more allegiance to the emperor of Japan than to the Tsar of Russia—were imprisoned for a long time, and a lot of them died in those camps, for no crime except that of being different. Well, that's all Steve Hansen is guilty of. Being different. He's got a good education. He likes to read. He doesn't know how to be ordinary. So he's the perpetual outsider, and that makes it easy to say he must be guilty of other things too. Well, he's not. I'm telling you, I'm damn near certain this man *is not* guilty of murder. I'm certain enough that I'd put him back in that uniform to stay if I thought I could pull it off. He didn't do it. He did *not* kill his wife and daughter. I don't care what a court said. I don't care what ten courts said. He didn't do it and I'm just about ready to prove he didn't. Now, Truax, maybe you've got the stomach to arrest a man you know isn't guilty because a piece of paper says to arrest him. I haven't. I don't care how many arrest warrants there are. I don't care how many convictions there are. I don't care how many death warrants there are. I won't arrest him if I know he's innocent. Now, I'll say it again. If you want to take him you take me too."

"Damn it, Shigata," Truax growled, "why didn't you say that to start with?"

"I tried to. You wouldn't listen."

"You tried to after I'd seen him. Why didn't you say it before I saw him?"

"Because Quinn and I already look like giraffes."

"What's that supposed to mean?"

"It means we've got our necks stuck out. We're risking our jobs, maybe our freedom. I have the right to run my own risks. I tried to keep Quinn out of it, but I couldn't. I didn't want anybody else in it. Including you. I don't know how elastic your conscience is and which way."

"Shigata, I don't want to burn an innocent man any more than you do. If you can prove it, then let's prove it."

"Fine. But right now we've got a crime scene to work."

Truax looked at Hansen. "I hope he's right. I hope he can prove it. All right, what did you find?"

"This," Hansen said. "I didn't touch them."

Shigata squatted. "Hot damn," he said. "There's about a one-tenth of one percent chance we might get prints off 'em."

"Brass?" Truax said, looking down at the empty cartridge cases. "You were looking for brass?"

"We were hoping for a slug," Shigata said. "But brass is a start." He pointed the camera straight down.

"Shigata, you know what?" Hansen said, looking at the ground.

"No, what?"

"Maybe you can prove I didn't kill Lillian and Gaylene. I hope you can. But you can't prove I didn't do this one. So that brass doesn't match either of my guns, so what? We can't prove the brass is connected to the killing, and anyway I might have another gun."

"I don't have to prove you didn't," Shigata said, nudging the spent brass into a plastic evidence bag. "Somebody else has to prove you did, if that's what they want to do. And I don't think they can."

"That's the theory," Hansen said. "It's a pretty theory. I learned the truth of it a few years back."

"The situation was a little different," Shigata said. "In more ways than you realize." He looked up from the squatting position. "Hansen, what would you say if I told you that Shipp knew to start with that your pistol wasn't the one used to kill them? And that he knew what pistol *had* been used?"

"You're saying he did it. Shigata, I saw him that morning, and I'm telling you he was in shock."

"Wouldn't you be if you'd just committed murder and were terrified that your frame job might not work? Think about it—all you needed was a good alibi. How could he know you hadn't gone and spent the night with some woman? That, of course, was why he had a second string to his bow, in case the first didn't work out."

"What are you talking about?"

"I'd rather show you than tell you. But right now—"

"Who's coming from the medical examiner's office?" Hansen asked suddenly.

"I don't know," Shigata said. "Probably Joel Moran or Bob Mann. Why? You want me to find out?"

"Yeah," Hansen said. "Because if it's Moran, I need to disappear. Mann I don't know."

"There's a saying," Quinn said. "Three people can keep a secret if two of 'em are dead. This secret's already up to four. Shigata, I'm telling you—"

"Shigata," Truax interrupted, "You better listen to your sergeant—uh, captain. Sorry, Quinn. Shigata, you can't do this."

"I can't do what?"

"You can't do what you're doing. Somebody with a law degree and FBI training ought to know better. Ought to, hell, you *do* know better. Running Hansen around dressed as a—"

"I had a reason," Shigata interrupted. "I'm not planning to keep him in uniform. But I've already—"

"Told me at great length how you feel about putting an innocent man in prison. Yeah. Right. I feel that way too. But I'm also sworn to obey the laws, and so are you."

"And so am I, if it comes to that," Hansen said softly. "The fact that I don't have the job anymore doesn't necessarily cancel the oath I took."

"You had a reason," Truax interrupted. "What reason?"

"Never mind what reason. I had one. I agree it's time to get him out of uniform now. But I don't want to lock him back up, and—"

"Shigata," Truax interrupted again, "your problem is you were a fed too long. You don't know well enough how cities and states do things."

84

"You may be right," Shigata said. "But what—"

"Now, here's what you do, Shigata," Truax went on. "Just call Huntsville. Tell them you've got Hansen in custody here in Galveston County. You want to hold him here long enough to finish investigating this killing, because you're pretty sure it was done by the same person that killed this woman's sister. You are, aren't you?"

"Not necessarily," Shigata said. "But there's a good chance—"

"Well, if you want to take a prisoner with you while you're investigating, that's your business. It's been done before. And if you think your jail is inadequate, then, where you put a prisoner is your business too, as long as you're sure it's secure. I mean, a motel room is plenty secure enough for somebody who doesn't intend to go anywhere anyway. You don't, do you, Hansen?"

"No," Hansen said.

"If I let Huntsville know, sooner or later Huntsville is going to send somebody—"

"Huntsville is going to send somebody after me sooner or later anyway," Hansen interrupted. "We've already talked about that. Shigata, I'm not being suicidal now, and I'm not playing martyr. I'm talking fact. Even when the proof turns up, it's still going to take time to get anything done. I'll be spending more time inside, and there's nothing any of us can do about it. Just—" He shook his head. "I can't honestly say I can't take it, because I can. I've lived with three years of it already. But if worse comes to worst—if it becomes evident nothing is going to change—I'm going to try to run. I'm going to try to run knowing I can't get anywhere. Will one of you aim carefully before pulling the trigger? And that's not being suicidal," he added. "If they're going to kill me anyway, I'd rather pick my own time."

"I can't do that," Shigata said.

"Truax?"

"No."

"Quinn?"

Quinn was silent. Then, finally, he shook his head. "I

can't. But I can slip you a pistol and walk off and leave you if it comes to that. I don't think it's going to."

"So we're agreed this is the way we're going?" Truax asked. "You'll let Huntsville know, and—"

Shigata began, "Not unless it's okay with—"

"It's okay with me," Hansen interrupted. "Shigata, he's right. You've got to do it."

"Okay, you're in custody," Shigata said. "Al, can you stay out here and look for—"

"Yeah," Quinn interrupted.

"I'll help," Truax said.

"We'll be back," Shigata said. "If you haven't found anything—"

"Yeah," Quinn said. "Go before the ME's team gets here."

Hansen swung into the passenger's seat of the Bronco and glanced over at the set of Shigata's jaw. "Don't worry about it," he said. "It's not your fault. It's not your doing. If you can help me, great. You may not be able to get me off. Could be nobody can. It's a tight frame. If you can't—at least you're trying. And that's more than anybody did when it happened."

"I know," Shigata said. "It's just—the man who did this to you used to wear the same badge I'm wearing now. It makes me sick. The whole idea. It makes me sick."

"At least he's not still wearing it."

"True."

"Maybe you'd feel better if you bought a new badge?"

That made Shigata laugh. "Maybe. Maybe. What do we need to get you in the way of clothes?"

"You've got plenty of jail coveralls. At least we used to."

"Piss on that. What do you need?"

"Nothing. A trip to the laundromat, maybe. They took my locker key away from me without allowing me time to clean out my locker. The entire locker contents was packed into a couple of boxes in the supply room. With four people and only two bathrooms at home, and Gaylene sort of lived in one of them, if you know how teenage girls are—"

"I have one," Shigata agreed. "And just one bathroom."

86

"Then you know. So to cut down on congestion I usually showered and shaved in the locker room, and I'd just put stuff back in it the day before—the day before. Razor, toothbrush, clean underwear, a couple of pair of jeans, T-shirts. No jacket, of course, it was the middle of summer, but that jacket I bought in Galveston is good enough. How'd you think I managed to shave when I was getting into uniform?"

"I figured Quinn had loaned you a razor."

"I was glad to find that stuff. I hadn't brushed my teeth in two days. Talk about feeling grungy!"

"Now I've got to see how I can pay for your motel room—"

"That's not your responsibility."

"I don't mean me, I mean the city."

"It's still not your responsibility."

"Hansen," Shigata said, "if the former chief of police of Bayport deliberately set you up—and I'm inclined to think he did—then the city owes you three and a half years of salary plus punitive damages."

"I'm not going to ask for it. All I want is my freedom and my job. As for the motel room, don't worry about it. I've got a little money stashed back."

"Same place the gun was stashed?"

"Yeah."

"You want to tell me now where it is? You don't have to."

Hansen told him. "You're going to have to register me," he added. "There's not a motel in town I'd feel safe walking into."

In looks, the police station hadn't changed at all in the time he'd been gone. Every step he took reminded him, painfully vividly, of the past. It seemed impossible that Dale Shipp wasn't going to step out of one of those doors with that ugly smile he had; it seemed impossible that Dan Buchanan wasn't still alive. Hansen paused outside the locker room, thumbs hitched in the top of his gunbelt, to read the bulletin board in the hall. *Check new bulletins every day. If you don't, you won't know what's happening. You*

87

tell it to all the rookies. Check the bulletin board every day. Especially if you've been off for a couple of days, because it's important to know what happened those days.

A soft voice spoke behind him. "Steve Hansen?"

He whirled, heart pounding, because nobody with a female voice was supposed to know where he was.

It was the blond, the one that was the watch commander. He searched her face. "How'd you know me?"

She smiled. "Think about it."

He thought about it. And then he said, "Claire. Claire. You used to baby-sit my kids. That was ten years ago. I'm sorry, I don't remember your last name."

"Barndt. What are you doing here, dressed like that?"

"I used to be—"

"I know what you used to be. I know what you are now."

"Do you? Are you sure?"

"Yes. I'm sure."

"Then what am I now?"

"You're not a killer," she said.

"That's what I'm not. So what am I? You said you know what I am, what am I?"

"Not what. Who. You're Steve Hansen. Of course." She stepped a little closer to him. "I had a crush on you when I was a kid, you know."

"No. I didn't know."

"Has it been pretty bad these last few years?"

"Yeah," he said. "You could say that."

"So what happens now?"

"Shigata thinks he can get me out. I hope he's right."

"He's pretty smart," Claire said.

"Yeah. I hope so."

"Law degree and all. And he believes in justice. He's nearly fifty years old, and he still believes in justice. Isn't that funny?"

"Yeah," Hansen said. "Real funny. I'm nearly fifty years old too. And I used to believe in justice. I used to think it was possible. Not recently, of course."

"No. Not recently. We all start out the same way."

88

"We?"

"Police. All of us. We all start out the same way. Except the ones like Shipp, of course. Did you know Shipp? He was chief when I first got on. I didn't like him."

"Yes. I knew Shipp."

"He started out asking what was in it for him. He was probably that way in his cradle. But the rest of us—you and me and Shigata and Quinn—we start out thinking of ourselves as knights in shining armor on milk-white steeds, out to save the world. And one day you wake up and you realize the world doesn't want to be saved. It just wants to be left alone to go to hell in its own way. I'm thinking about joining the FBI. Or maybe the Secret Service."

"So you can leave the world to go to hell in a handcart," Hansen gibed. "Right. You're young to be so cynical."

"Were you cynical when you were my age?"

"I was born cynical. What's your excuse?"

"You weren't, you know."

"I wasn't what?"

"Born cynical. It doesn't come naturally to you. I used to read your books at night after the kids were asleep."

"Did you?" *I wonder what became of my books.*

"Yes. Sometimes you reminded me of Don Quixote."

He laughed. "Did I? How's that?"

"All those beautiful books. And you were out tilting at windmills because the books said you could win, and every time the windmills knocked you over, you got back up again."

"Till this time."

"This time isn't over," Claire said.

"So you still think right can win over might?"

"Well," she said, and didn't finish.

Hansen leaned over her and touched her lips with his, very gently, not touching anywhere else. "That was nice," he said.

"Yes . . . but not enough."

"No," he said. "Not enough. I've got to go change clothes now, before Shigata comes looking for me."

"I heard somebody found Shelley Morgan."

"Yeah. Somebody found Shelley Morgan."

"Has anybody notified Todd?"

His young face was suffused with rage. "You said you weren't going to kill Shelley."

"I didn't kill Shelley," Hansen said.

"Then who did!" Todd shouted. "Who else had any reason to? I don't believe you— you made me believe you, that you didn't kill Mom and Gaylene, but now—" He turned to Shigata. "Can't you get him away from here? Can't you make him go away?"

"Todd, please listen to me—"

"I did listen to you! I listened to you yesterday and I didn't call the cops about you, and now—"

"What would it take," Hansen asked wearily, "for me to convince you I didn't do it, then or now?"

"Nothing. You can't. You did it."

"Todd—" Shigata began.

"I don't want to listen to you either. All you cops stick together. Everybody knows that."

"That's not true," Shigata said. "There is nothing and nobody police officers hate more than a police officer who has gone bad."

"He used to say that too. That was before he killed my mother."

"Where's Shelley's address book?" Hansen asked.

"What do you want that for?" Todd demanded, his voice shrill. "You want to find somebody else to kill?"

"I want to call your aunt Marion. Somebody has to take care of you."

"And formally identify Shelley's body," Shigata said.

"I can do that," Hansen said. "I'm officially here now, remember?"

"Oh, yeah, that's right," Shigata said.

"I can take care of myself," Todd said.

"You're sixteen," Hansen pointed out.

"What difference does it make? I can take care of myself."
Todd looked at Shigata. "You haven't even arrested him.

90

You're just letting him run around like—"

"I'm in custody," Hansen interrupted. "Somebody from Huntsville can come get me and take me back any time they like."

"So when are they gonna kill you?"

"When they get ready to, I suppose."

"I'll be glad."

"Fine," Hansen said. "That's your privilege. In the meantime, get me Shelley's address book."

"Todd—" Shigata began again.

"I said I don't want to listen to you."

"You're damn well going to listen to me. When I am able to show who really did these killings—and I hope it won't be long before I can—I hope you'll have the decency to apologize to your father."

Todd stood up and stalked off, slamming his bedroom door hard.

"He's under a lot of strain," Hansen said.

"He doesn't deserve to have you defend him."

"Believe it or not," Hansen said, "he was a happy kid. Until all this happened. He was a happy kid. We used to— Never mind." He wiped tears out of his eyes. "You want to call Marion, or do you want me to?"

"She anything like Shelley?"

"No. Todd would have been better off with her, but she's got five kids of her own, and I guess the court didn't figure she had room to take on another."

"I'll call her," Shigata said.

Todd stalked back into the living room, slouched into a chair, and ostentatiously picked up the *TV Guide*.

"It all looks so easy on TV," Hansen said. "You find out in an hour who did it, you never make mistakes, and all the loose ends are neatly tied up."

"And nobody gets left holding the baby," Shigata agreed. "Hello? Mrs. Morrison? I'm the chief of police in Bayport—"

Chapter 7

"F<small>EEL LIKE EATING?</small>" Shigata asked.

"There's not a place in this town where people wouldn't know me. Not unless it opened up last week."

"You're legal. You're with me."

"I'm not in handcuffs and leg irons. Have you ever tried to sit down and eat in a room with people who used to be your friends and now think you killed your wife?"

"Actually," Shigata said, "I have. A year ago last October, my first wife—we'd been separated about six months, but we were still married—was bludgeoned to death in Galveston. The Galveston police decided I was It. And Quinn— that was when I first met Quinn—maneuvered me into going to lunch with Roy Hidalgo and Matt Dean."

Hansen whistled. "So how'd you get clear of that?"

"Found out who did it. And that's what we're going to do for you. I would take you home with me for lunch, but I told Melissa not to expect me today. And it's a hell of a long time past lunch anyway. If you want, we'll get sandwiches and take them into my office. But I think you'd feel better with a decent meal. Any preference where?"

After a little thought, Hansen asked, "Is Jack's still in business?"

"It was yesterday. Jack's it is."

The little truck-stop restaurant was almost empty at this time on a Sunday. The owner, Jack Horan, stepped out from behind the counter armed with menus, and then stopped. "Sergeant Hansen?"

Hansen nodded. "Yeah. But not sergeant. Not anymore."

Horan looked accusingly at Shigata, then looked back at Hansen. "I heard you'd escaped. I hoped you'd get away clean."

"I wasn't trying to. Anyway, where would I go?"

"Mexico, maybe? If you weren't trying, then why—"

"To have a shot at whoever killed my wife," Hansen said softly.

"You could've let him do that, Chief Shigata," Horan said. There was deep reproach in his voice, in his emphasis on "that."

"We're working on it," Shigata answered. "So you don't think Sergeant Hansen—"

"A lot of lying went on at that trial," Horan interrupted. "I wanted to be a character witness, but they wouldn't let me."

"Who wouldn't let you?" Hansen asked sharply.

"That young ass of a lawyer you had, that's who. Wouldn't let me testify, wouldn't even let me talk to you."

"He never told me," Hansen said. "He was court-appointed. I didn't like him, but the judge said I couldn't have anybody else unless I could pay the bills myself, and obviously I couldn't. He never told me anybody wanted to speak for me. I thought everybody in this town was against me."

"A lot of lying went on at that trial," Horan repeated. "A lot of people were ready to speak for you, but they didn't get a chance. If you could get a decent lawyer, maybe a new trial—"

"He's got a better lawyer," Shigata said. "He'll get a new trial."

"That's good to hear. Your usual, then Sergeant?" Horan said, pencil poised over pad.

"Yes. Please."

"And you, Chief Shigata?"

"The same. Whatever it is. I'm game."

After Horan departed for the kitchen, Hansen asked, "And just who is this better lawyer I've got?"

"Me," Shigata said.

Hansen looked at him.

"I'm a qualified member of the bar in Texas and several other states," Shigata said. "Admittedly, I've never actually practiced law. But I can. If I want to. And right now I think I want to."

"Conflict of interest? Who's the prosecuting witness?"

"Well, now, that does seem to be a problem," Shigata said. "How are they going to hold a trial if nobody shows up to testify against you? They might just have to dismiss the case altogether. Who was it last time? Shipp?"

"Shipp," Hansen confirmed. "Sitting right there beside the prosecuting attorney, grinning that spiteful grin of his every time I turned my head."

"Shipp's not going to appear again. He'll be behind bars by then."

"Buchanan, then."

"I told you Buchanan's dead. Henry Samford shot him. I shot Henry Samford."

"DOA?" Hansen asked.

"DOA," Shigata confirmed. "Very DOA. Quinn shot him too."

Hansen broke a cracker in two pieces and went on breaking it, methodically, until it was entirely crumbs. He swept the crumbs neatly into the ashtray. "They must've broken out the beer kegs in hell when Samford showed up."

"You knew Samford?"

"He killed that baby of his. Reported her kidnapped. She wasn't kidnapped. He killed her. Buried her in the backyard. I know that as well as I know the sun is shining. But I never could get enough for a search warrant. His wife was scared to talk. Not that I blame her. Son of a bitch was a sadist. God only knows what he put her through. Whatever became of her afterward?"

"I married her," Shigata said.

94

"You married her."

"Yes. I married her. Anything wrong with that?"

Hansen shook his head. "Your business is your business."

"But you lived in this town twenty years. Policed in this town twenty years."

"Right," Hansen said.

"And you're not sure I knew what I was getting into."

"I didn't say that."

"I've seen her rap sheet. I know what happened to her. I know why it happened. What's past is past."

"That's what I thought when I married Lillian. Until the past stood up and hit me in the face."

"The difference is, Samford's dead," Shigata said.

"Yeah," Hansen said, "there's that. Too bad Shipp isn't."

"We're working on that. What I wonder right now is, who else wanted to testify for you and wasn't allowed to?"

Hansen shrugged. "GOK."

"We'll find out."

"Right now what I want to know is what makes you so sure you can pin it on Shipp. I know you said you'd show me. But the day is moving on. Tell me."

"You were told that .357 was the murder weapon. It wasn't."

"So you said. But how do you figure—"

"It was sealed in an evidence bag," Shigata interrupted. "Shipp and Buchanan both initialed the bag and put the date and time on it, quite properly. The pistol was collected at your house and the bag was stapled at your house. And it was never reopened. Therefore, no test firing was ever made from that firearm."

"Shigata—" Hansen began, "I told you—"

"That Shipp didn't claim he'd fired a test shot. I know. But the three loaded cartridges were loaded with your soft-lead bullets with the X carved in the nose. The three empties matched them. Copper jackets and plain lead bullets don't usually come in the same package."

"But—"

"And you were told there were no usable prints on the gun. That wasn't true. There were good prints. But before those prints got on, the pistol had been wiped clean of fingerprints. Totally clean. You know as well as I do a pistol is never clean of fingerprints. And then somebody after wiping it clean had put a left thumbprint on the trigger and left forefinger, ring finger, and middle finger on the back-strap. Suicide position. Only it hadn't been used for suicide, because it wasn't the fatal weapon at all. So somebody else put those prints on the gun after Lillian was dead."

"You haven't read the trial transcript," Hansen said. He glanced at Horan, who was putting plates on the table. "Thanks, Jack. You want to sit down and join us?"

"I'm working on tomorrow's barbecue," Horan said. "And you're working. I can see that."

"Shigata," Hansen said, moving a slice of roast beef around on his plate, "you weren't at the trial. You haven't seen the trial transcripts."

"That's true. I haven't.

"Did you read the local reports? Shipp's and Buchanan's?"

"There weren't any there from Buchanan. I read Shipp's reports. Such as they were. If I had an officer who wrote reports like that, I'd send him—or her—to College of the Mainland to learn how to write."

"You couldn't get him in. Shipp's not much more than borderline literate. But he's shrewd. He's shrewd. Now, let me tell you what he did."

"Okay." Shigata poked, rather doubtfully, at the glob of slightly overcooked green leaves on his plate.

"It's collards," Hansen said. "You don't have to like it. Most people don't if they weren't born in the South. Okay. I'll have to give you some background. My house was right on the edge of town; in fact, when I bought it it was outside the city limits, and then the city limits moved. There weren't any neighbors at all to the back of us, just a flat open field. You could see farther than you could shoot with a handgun. So I built a frame and hauled up some sand and made a firing range with a target butt in my backyard. I used to practice out there a lot. I taught Gaylene and Todd to shoot. I wanted to teach Lillian, but she refused to try."

"I thought you told me Todd didn't know how to shoot."

"No, I told you he didn't have a gun. I wouldn't buy him a BB gun or an air rifle, because so many kids try to use them as toys. Neither they nor their parents realize the damn things are dangerous. At thirteen he wasn't old enough to own a gun, and I don't think a gun is anything you give to a kid anyway. I just owned the two handguns, and I kept whichever one I wasn't carrying locked up along with my rifle and shotgun. Anyhow, every so often I'd sift through the sand and collect all the lead and take it to a fellow I knew in LaMarque who did reloading. I mostly used wadcutters for target shooting, of course."

"Of course," Shigata said. There is a considerable difference in cost between a box of fifty new cartridges and a box of fifty reloaded wadcutters.

"So Shipp and the DA—this was a real young assistant DA, and he was kind of following Shipp's lead—didn't introduce the pistol into evidence until after the firearms examiner from Austin had testified and left. Shipp told the jury he hadn't test-fired that gun because he had reason to believe I might have used a different pistol for the murder and left that one on the floor as a smoke screen to distract attention from the real murder weapon."

"So you told me," Shigata said. "You also told me, and I agree, that that's a load of crap. Didn't your lawyer object?"

"Yes, but the judge overruled him. Shipp said instead of firing a test shot that might have been totally misleading, he went out to the butt behind my house and dug in the sand. And he did. Neighbors saw him doing it. They were brought in to testify. So was Dan Buchanan, who was with him when he did it. He said he collected the particular test slug he collected because it was a copper jacket and the fatal slugs were copper jackets. He produced neighbors to say they'd often seen me back there shooting at the butts and that they'd seen me using different pistols at different times. Which, of course, they had. I have two pistols, and you know yourself there's a lot of difference between firing a two-inch barrel and firing a five-inch barrel. I practiced with both."

Shigata nodded, and then asked, "Who besides you and your kids had used the butt?"

"Different people at different times. Probably just about the whole department. Buchanan came out there several times. For that matter, Shipp came out himself at least once. Maybe twice. But they had chased down the fellow who was doing the reloading, and he testified as to when the last time was that I had brought him lead and brass for reloading. The neighbors swore they hadn't seen anybody but me back there since then."

"Had they?"

"No, because Shipp and Buchanan came out when the neighbors weren't home. If the copper jackets weren't fired out of my gun, then Shipp or Buchanan, one or the other, fired that copper jacket into my target. But I can't prove it."

"I still don't understand why you think Lillian shot herself?"

"Because I still don't see another answer."

Shigata shook his head. "Let me get back to the trial, then," he said. "Basically what the jury was told was that the prosecution did not necessarily contend that you had shot Lillian and Gaylene with your service revolver, but that you had shot her with a pistol—that one or another one— that you had first sighted in by test firing it behind your house."

"That's right."

"What did you think of that?"

"I thought it was a load of crap. But I didn't see any sense in arguing about it. It was my gun, and I really did think it was suicide."

"I'll ask you again. Why did you feel that way?"

"Because I couldn't see any other answer that made sense. And I still can't. Except that if it wasn't my gun, then there must be some other answer."

"Hansen, given all this, isn't it easier to think Shipp did it than to think Lillian did?"

98

The front door of the café opened, and a woman entered. She didn't look threatening to Shigata—just a woman in late middle age, heavily built, wearing a little too much makeup—but she stopped abruptly just inside the door. That was the only reason Shigata noticed her, that and the fact that, like any cop, he always noticed who came in through doors.

But then he glanced at Hansen. Hansen was sitting quite still, quite silent, looking at her, and there was something in his eyes Shigata wouldn't like to feel directed at him. The woman looked back at him, lips pulling back from her teeth in what certainly was not a smile. The expression that crept across her face combined anger, fear—something else. Something else Shigata couldn't read, any more than he could read what was on Hansen's face.

"Hello, Celeste," Hansen drawled, in a voice that didn't quite shake but wasn't quite steady either.

She turned and left, quickly, the screen door clattering shut behind her.

"You don't know her?" Hansen asked.

Shigata shook his head. "Should I?"

"Celeste Shipp," Hansen explained. "Dale Shipp's wife. And I guarantee you, what she knows, he knows. She's off now to report to hubby. Well. Where were we?"

"I was asking you if it wouldn't be easier to believe—"

"Oh, yeah, that Shipp did it, not Lillian. It would be," Hansen said, "if I hadn't seen him that morning. And if I could figure out how Shipp would know I was gone from home. I'd rather believe that."

"You said you went to a bar in Galveston?"

"That's right."

"Had you ever been there before?"

"Two or three times, I guess. Not often. I couldn't afford to drink much, and most of the time I wanted to be with my family if I wasn't on duty. But I have a hell of a temper. I felt it was better, when I lost it, to get out of the house rather than stick around and risk saying or doing something I'd regret later. Lillian agreed with me."

"Was there anybody at the bar you knew?"

"No. I wish there had been. I'd probably have talked more and drunk less and gone home that night."

"Had you ever stayed gone all night before?"

"No. That was the only time I ever did it."

"Did you have one car or two?"

"Just one. It was really all we needed. When Lillian needed the car, either she dropped me by the station or I'd have the beat car swing by and pick me up."

"How recognizable was it?"

He shrugged. "It was a yellow Pinto. How distinctive do you think a yellow Pinto is?"

"When you parked at home, could anybody see the car from the street?"

"Yes, easily."

"So if somebody drove by at night and the lights were on and the car was gone they could reasonably assume you weren't there?"

"Yes," Hansen said, "but they couldn't conclude I wouldn't be back soon. Unless I was on duty."

"The last thing in the world Shipp wanted was to pull this when you were on duty," Shigata said. "Did anybody know you had a habit of going to sit on the beach when you were upset? Or was it a habit?"

"It was a habit. And yes, I guess just about everybody who knew me knew that. I used to quote Melville at people who asked me why."

"Did you usually use the same beach?"

"Yes, unless it was too crowded. I picked a place that wasn't, usually."

"Now, let's postulate something," Shigata said. "Postulate that the situation was as you think it was, and that Shipp knew it."

"Okay."

"And he knows Lillian well enough to know that she won't tell you, but you'll be able to tell she's upset and you'll try to get it out of her. Or if she does tell you, then you'll really be upset."

100

"If she had told me, I'd have been as like as not to go gunning for Shipp," Hansen admitted.

"Okay, so he drives past your house and sees you're not there. That means you and Lillian had a fight and you took off. It's late enough the bars would be closed, and anyway he knows you don't usually drink much. So he goes—or sends somebody—to see if you're parked on the beach. You are. At this point he may not know how much time he's got, but he knows he's got some. How long does it take to pull a trigger three times, wipe fingerprints off a different pistol and put new fingerprints on it, and take off?"

"Shigata, why in the world would anybody put fingerprints in a suicide position on a gun that wasn't used? That doesn't make sense even for Shipp."

"Then maybe Shipp didn't do that part of it. Maybe Buchanan helped him. Maybe Lillian got your gun herself, trying to fight back, and missed."

"She would've. She never would learn to shoot. But there weren't any extra bullet holes in the living room. And in that case, the gunpowder residue would have been positive."

"It isn't always," Shigata said. "You get a lot of false negatives."

"But nobody could count on getting one. I agree that Buchanan was about that stupid," Hansen went on. "Stupid enough not to know different pistols leave different marks on bullets. But he was a fairly good-natured fellow. I can't see him consenting to murder."

"Can't you?" Shigata asked grimly. "I can."

"You know something about Buchanan you haven't told me."

"I know a hell of a lot about Buchanan that I haven't told you," Shigata answered. "I know he was Henry Samford's toady, and I know he helped Samford commit murder. And tried to help Samford kill Quinn and me. But I don't know what kind of relationship there was between Shipp and Buchanan or, for that matter, between Shipp and Samford. Not that I think Samford was involved in this."

"He wouldn't have been. I'm a nice white Anglo-Saxon

Protestant. Samford didn't have anything against me—he didn't know I'd been trying to make a case on him—and I stayed out of his way. But if Buchanan was Samford's toady, that's news to me. When I was here, Shipp was Samford's toady and Buchanan was Shipp's."

"If Buchanan toadied for Shipp like he toadied for Samford," Shigata said, "there is literally nothing he wouldn't do if Shipp told him to."

"You speak as one who knows."

"I've got scars on my back from my shoulders to my waist that Samford and a few of his buddies put there. Buchanan helped him. So did Bob Kerns."

"Kerns? The fellow that used to run that gunshop, K and S?"

"The same."

"I shouldn't be surprised. But I'll admit I am. So Samford's dead and Buchanan's dead. I wouldn't want to have you mad at me. What about Kerns?"

"He's in Atlanta."

"Why Atlanta? Why not Huntsville?"

"I was still in the FBI when it happened. Assault on a federal officer."

Hansen thought about it. "I'm a little speechless," he said. "I mean, just to look at you, you look like somebody who's never had any trouble. You have that upper-middle-class bearing about you, like I used to have. But from what you say, it sounds like you've been through as much as Quinn. And I know more about him than he thinks I do. He used to drink. *In vino veritas.* He told me quite a bit about himself one night at an FOP party."

"He says the same thing about you."

"I did. We were both drunk. The only thing surprising is that both of us remember it."

"Maybe you weren't as drunk as you thought you were. Anyway, no, I wouldn't say I've been through as much as he has. But I've been through enough to know I don't want any more."

"I guess not. So who owns K and S now? Or has it shut down?"

102

"Dale Shipp owns it," Shigata said.

"Oh, *shit!*" Hansen's right hand balled into a fist. "Shigata, I can't prove I didn't ever own another pistol. I can't prove I wasn't sighting in another pistol out there behind my house. My only chance, my *only* chance, to get clear of this thing is to find the pistol those shots were fired from. You know that just as well as I do, even if you won't say it. So if Shipp has sold it—"

"We're going to find the slug that killed Shelley," Shigata said. "If it matches, then we know Shipp still has the gun. If it doesn't, well, we may be back to square one. If I have to call in the ATF to check all K and S's sales records. I'll do it."

"Shigata, that slug could be anywhere in a three-mile radius—"

"It could be. But wherever it was fired, there was a spray out the car window. The spray'll be on the side of the road. We'll find it if I have to borrow the National Guard to look for it."

"Yeah. Unless a dog licked it up. Unless Shipp got out of the car and threw a shovelful of dirt on it. Unless—"

"Stop it," Shigata said. "There was nobody in your corner last time. Now you've got Quinn and me, and I think Truax. You're not alone against the world. And with Samford and Buchanan dead, Shipp's got fewer people on his side. The odds are different."

"They need to be."

Jack Horan returned. "Sergeant Hansen, you want some pie?"

"Not this time. Thanks."

"It's on the house."

"I appreciate that. But not this time."

"You'll come back and get it later?"

"I hope so," Hansen said. "I damn sure hope so. And I may be calling on you to be a witness. You really won't mind?"

"I'll be there. Me and Milly both. You come back. Both of you. No, there's no ticket, this is on the house. Sergeant

Hansen used to be a good customer of mine. I want him back."

Truax and Quinn were still out in the middle of the field. "We'll relieve you," Shigata said. "Go get something to eat."

Quinn nodded. "My stomach thinks my throat's been cut. The blowout's right over there. Best as we can figure the trajectory, it came this way. Unless it hit something and ricocheted, and there wasn't anything for it to hit except her skull."

"I got pictures and collected samples already," Truax said. "I'm not officially here, but nobody'll mind. There were tire tracks. You could see where the car was parked when she was shot. I made plaster casts. I'll want the tires off the car. I'll run it all to Austin tomorrow. You got anything else you want to send?"

"Yeah," Shigata said. "I'm sending those slugs from the old case back, along with both of Hansen's pistols. The slugs didn't come from either one, but I want the lab to say so. I'm sending along those copper jackets from the box in my desk, to see if they can say the slugs came from the same manufacturer. And the box they were in, to see if Shipp's fingerprints are on it."

"You got Shipp's fingerprints?"

"The state ought to— No?" Truax was shaking his head.

"No. He was grandfathered. He was in before the state started checking prints on police applicants. And they didn't go back and check them from everybody that was already working."

"Then I hope there's a set in files. I sure don't have probable cause to get a court order demanding prints."

"Anything else?"

"The slug from this field. If we can find it."

"Lots of luck."

"You want me to call Galveston and ask them to bring up a couple of metal detectors?" Quinn asked.

"That's the best idea I've heard lately," Shigata said. "Unless—what is this?"

104

He was kneeling in the weeds as they spoke. "What is this?"

It was as gray as a pebble, except for the shiningly fresh fragmented edges of lead. Lead and copper, fused together.

And caught in the leading edge of the slug, a miniscule fragment of gleaming white.

Skull bone.

This was the slug.

Truax, who had a camera case slung around his neck, opened it. "I'll pace the distance off," Quinn said. He headed back toward the road, walking with a military-regulation thirty-inch stride.

"Anything else?" Truax inquired after nudging the slug into a plastic evidence envelope and labeling it.

"You're leaving tomorrow morning?"

"Yes."

"Just come by before you leave."

"I've got to. You haven't given me the pistols and slugs yet."

"I may have something more. You two go on and eat. We already did."

"So where are you going now?" Quinn asked.

"To check on some things," Shigata said. "And try to throw a scare into Shipp. If he thinks he's sitting tight, he'll go right on sitting tight. If he thinks we know more than we do, then he might be spooked into making a mistake. And I'm afraid that's the only way we're going to get him. Hansen, do you know who's living in your house now?"

Hansen shook his head. "The bank repossessed it. That's all I know. I couldn't even get the rest of my possessions out, because I was back in jail by then."

"Tell me the way. Or do you want to drive?"

"No driver's license. Shipp took it when I was arrested."

The yard was grown up in weeds that had been partly, but not totally, winter-killed by the brief frost. The sign in front said "For Sale by Bank." Hansen stood on the front porch for a minute. Then he stepped off the porch, reached up into the rain gutter, and dug a key out from the debris. He

105

unlocked the front door. "This is burglary, you know," he said over his shoulder.

"Illegal entry for the purpose of committing a felony? It's only trespassing. Unless you intend to commit a felony. If you do, warn me."

"A matter of interpretation," Hansen said. "I intend to remove some of my belongings. If they're salvageable. The bank might consider them the bank's belongings."

"Hansen, don't expect too much. We had a hell of a hurricane late last summer."

"Yeah. I see."

But the bookshelves were on an inside wall. Although the books smelled musty, they weren't actually wet. The framed photographs were water-spotted, but they were salvageable.

"Don't try to get anything now," Shigata said. "I'll help you get it back legally. Even if you do have to go back to Huntsville, we can get your things stored beforehand, so you'll have them later."

"Yeah," Hansen said. "I just wish I could get my family back that easily. What did we come here for?"

"I want a look at that target."

"I'll show you the way." Hansen relocked the house. Then, with a slightly defiant glance at Shigata, he put the key inside his billfold, behind a flap in the bill section.

The firing range was overgrown with beach grass now. The sand butt had collapsed a little, but there was no indication anybody had touched it in years. "I want to get some slugs out of there, but I can't do it now. I'll have to come back with a search warrant," Shigata said.

"I'll give— Oh. I can't give consent. It's not mine anymore."

"Right. But that doesn't matter. You've said enough to give me probable cause any judge will respect."

"Chief Shigata," Hansen said in the car, "this has been a crazy day. Six hours ago I was pointing a gun at your head, and you've done everything you can think of ever since to help me."

"You thought you were pointing a gun at Dale Shipp's head. And I really have no particular quarrel with that. I just want to make sure whatever happens to Shipp happens legally."

"Yeah. This day feels like it's been about two years long."

"I know what you mean. You ready for some rest?"

"Yes."

"Is Bartlett's Motel good enough?"

"Yes. It's cheap and quiet. Shigata, I policed a long time, but I don't have any more knowledge of the law than you have to have to police in a small town. Realistically, what would you say my chances are of beating all this?"

Shigata concentrated on driving. "Better than fifty-fifty," he said finally. "If we can get Todd back on your side, it'll go up."

"If frogs had wings, they wouldn't bump their backsides when they hop."

"True. I'll go check you in. Any preferred alias?"

"S. R. Hanson." He spelled the last name. "The *R* really is my middle initial. And enough people spell Hansen with an *O*. Bartlett might guess. I don't think he will."

"I'll see to it he doesn't."

Hansen was alone—legally—for the first time in longer than he could easily remember. Quinn and Shigata knew where he was. Both watch commanders knew where he was, in case someone from Huntsville showed up prematurely for him, but in that case Shigata intended to try everything he could think of to send the representative from Huntsville back empty-handed.

He was trying to figure out how it felt to be legally alone. He was next door to the laundry room, so he'd already washed and dried clothes. He had three days' worth of clean underwear in a drawer. He had three pair of jeans (one of them stamped inside with the name of the prison), four shirts, and a clean if somewhat frayed jacket hanging up. He also had— at Shigata's insistence, not his—his own six sergeant's uniforms and his gunbelt, with the .357 still in it.

Claire thinks I'm Don Quixote. How good a look has she taken at her chief?

He had sandwiches, cookies, milk, and Cokes from the closest 7-Eleven. He had a telephone, if there was anybody he wanted to call, and a color television, if there was anything he wanted to watch.

He didn't want to use either. Todd wouldn't talk to him if he did call over there, and he'd been able to watch television in his cell. So that was nothing new. He'd had a shower and he'd unmade the bed to lie down between clean smooth sheets, but he wasn't sleepy. He was too tired and too keyed-up and too numb from all that had happened. Even *Pale Fire* was momentarily failing to hold his interest.

Somebody knocked on the door. He tensed. "Who is it?" he called.

"Just me. Claire. Can I come in?"

"Just a minute. Let me get some pants on."

"You didn't have to," she said when he opened the door. She was already in uniform, although it was only nine-thirty and, unless there'd been a lot of changes made in shift arrangements, she didn't go on duty until eleven-thirty.

"I preferred to." He stepped away from the door. "Why are you here?"

"I wanted to visit you."

"That's nice." He sat back down on the bed, leaving the only chair for her.

He couldn't think of anything else to say. Apparently she couldn't either, because she sat and fidgeted for a couple of minutes.

Then she said, "I brought you a present."

"That's nice of you. What?"

She tossed him a small plastic bag from Rexall. He opened it, curiously, and pulled out a small rectangular box labeled "Trojans."

He sat holding it for a moment. Then he glanced at Claire. She was blushing slightly, with her eyes fixed on him to watch what he would do.

"Claire, I'm very nearly twice your age," he said gently.

108

"What difference does that make?"

"None to you. Some to me. Claire—Claire—don't make me want to hold on to life now, when I'm trying to let go of it. I want to feel less now, not more. I'm under sentence of death."

"We're all under sentence of death, from the time we're born. I don't know what's going to happen on the street tonight."

"That's different. Dying hot, you don't have time to think about it. Dying cold, where you know a week ahead of time you're going to die on November eighth at eleven o' clock in the morning, that's different. I got over being afraid to die. I have so little left to lose, you see. Don't give me a reason now to dread the end."

" *'To love that well which thou must leave ere long'?* "

"Where did you find that?"

"In one of your books. Ten years ago. You had it marked. It made me cry."

"And you've remembered it. Shakespeare's seventy-third sonnet. *That time of year thou may'st in me behold—*"

"I didn't remember the rest of it."

"I do. Claire, is this because I've been sentenced to die, or in spite of it?"

"Does it matter?"

"It does to me. I don't want this because of your pity."

"Who mentioned pity? I didn't. Have you been in prison so long you've forgotten you're a very desirable man?"

Hansen stood up and laid the box on the table. "We don't need these," he said. "I—uh—had minor surgery thirteen years ago."

Claire stood up, took her gunbelt off, and laid it on the dresser beside his.

When she slipped quietly out at ten-forty-five, wearing the wrong gunbelt because she'd dressed in the dark, Hansen was deeply asleep.

Chapter 8

AFTER LEAVING HANSEN AT the motel, Shigata didn't go directly home. He stopped first at his office to call the bank president and see whether he could get a consent search for Hansen's former house.

"I don't see why not," Gene Taylor said. "I mean, if it's okay with Hansen."

"He doesn't own the place anymore," Shigata said patiently. Explaining legalities to laymen could get complicated.

"If he's innocent—and I hope he is—I'll work with him to find a way for him to get the place back. If he wants it, that is. I mean, he'd been paying for fifteen years on a twenty-year loan. I hated to foreclose, but I have to answer to the stockholders."

"It's okay with Hansen. If you'll just let me run by and get you to sign this—"

"I'll sign it, but I want to write on it that it has to be okay with Hansen too."

"That's fine."

It was almost dark when he got back to the Hansen house, this time with Quinn. "You want to search in the dark?" Quinn asked dubiously.

"We're hunting lead. You can do that by feel."

"Me? What are you going to be doing?"

"*We* can do that by feel."

"Yow!" Quinn said once, forty-five minutes into the task.

"What?" Shigata said. His back was aching from the awkward position.

"A cat's been in here."

"Not lately, I hope."

"Not lately. I should have expected it. Sand. Cats like sand."

Shigata chuckled and went on shifting sand between his fingers.

"I guess it'll be a lot easier for you," Quinn commented, "once we get Hansen back."

"I've been thinking about that," Shigata said, "and I'm not sure it will. Problem is, I've got to be on in the daytime, I need you on in the daytime, and I've got to put Hansen on days until he gets that boy of his straightened up. So that still leaves swing and deep nights uncovered. As long as we have Barlow and Barndt, we're halfway covered. But you're probably right that Barndt's about to bail out, and obviously for anything big they've got to call you or me or both of us anyway."

"I can work deep nights."

"When do you propose to sleep?"

"I'll manage," Quinn said.

"Maybe I can work out something with split shifts. Things are usually pretty dead from two A.M. till about four-thirty or five."

"Anyway, that wasn't what I meant."

"Then what did you mean? I'm sorry. I must not be following you."

"I meant education. You and Hansen both have about eight years of college. I've got about three years of high school. You'll have somebody around here you can talk with."

"I'd never noticed any difficulty communicating with you."

"You know what I mean. I was thinking, too, Hansen's got a lot more street experience than I do, so if you wanted to make him captain and move me back down to sergeant—"

"Al," Shigata said, "there are three things you need to know. First, I don't pick friends on the basis of proximity."

"What does that mean?"

"You know what the hell I mean. And I know what you mean, and I don't particularly appreciate it. Second, I don't promote people on the basis of friendship. If I got you a promotion to captain, it was because I damn well felt you deserved it. And third, I don't demote people except for cause. Nuff said?"

"Nuff said," Quinn answered, "but that may not be fair to Hansen."

"I don't know Hansen well enough to know that yet. I'll take care of that situation when it arises. Obviously I can't do anything about it until then. I think this is all we're going to get out of here."

"I think so too. You found any copper jackets?"

"I can't tell by feel. I might have one. I might also have some cat you-know-what."

"I know I do. The cat shat on lead."

"Careless of the cat."

"Cats are like that," Quinn said. "Inconsiderate. I never did like cats."

"That must be why you have three of them."

"Not me. The kids. Anyway, it's seven."

"You have kittens again?"

"Not me," Quinn said. "The cat. You want a kitten?"

"I expect I'm getting one no matter what I say."

"Well, Gail seems to want one."

"That's what I figured."

It had taken well over an hour to demolish the sand butt and collect every chunk of lead—and every pebble and seashell, because by then neither Shigata nor Quinn could see the difference—in it. "What now?" Quinn asked wearily.

"Now I take you home so you can get some sleep. You can't work twenty-four hours a day."

"What are you going to do?"

"I'm going to go scare Dale Shipp."

112

"Sure you don't need a backup?"

"If you can't find me tomorrow, you know where to start looking. No, I don't need a backup. Quinn, for crying out loud, go home and get some rest."

"Include me on this one," Quinn said.

"I'm not trying to shut you out. It's just that you're so damned tired, and you've got your mind full of some sort of personal problem—"

"Which does not affect you and does not affect my work."

"Anything that affects you affects your morale, and that affects your work and that affects me. I'll drop you by your house and—"

Quinn lifted the bag of lead, pebbles, and cat droppings into the back of the Bronco. "Shigata," he said, "you told me, back before you ever left the FBI, that if I saw you making a mistake you wanted me to tell you."

"So I did," Shigata said warily.

"I should have called you on letting Hansen run around in uniform. That was the kind of stupid that gives stupid a bad name."

"You're right. It was. But I wanted to see what he'd do about that pistol. I needed to know."

"And this time I *am* calling you. I won't let you go by yourself to try to scare Shipp. That son of a bitch is tougher than mule hide. He could take you or me either one, alone. But he can't take us both together, and so he won't try."

Shigata slammed the car door and put the keys in the ignition.

"Either my advice is worth something to you or it's not," Quinn said conversationally. "But either way I'm not letting you go to Shipp's place alone. If you drop me by my house, I'll just get in my car and follow you."

Shigata backed the Bronco out of the driveway. "Okay," he said. "You're right. I don't like it, but then, I don't have to like it. But after we get through rattling Shipp's cage, I'm taking you home and you're going to stay there and get some rest if I have to tell Nguyen to take your car keys and hide them."

"You don't have to tell her," Quinn said. "She's done it before."

I'm dead on my feet, Shigata thought. *I got up this morning at four-thirty, and it's past seven at night now. I'm good for a few more hours, but not as many as I'd have been good for ten years ago. Quinn is older than I am, and he's been up well over twenty-four hours. What do I have to do to talk this guy into resting?*

But he's right. I don't have any business going by myself to rattle Shipp's cage.

"That's a big house," Shigata observed, stopping where Quinn told him to.

"Yeah. Hadn't you seen it before?"

"No. I hadn't had any occasion to."

"Well," Quinn said, "think about this. Up until he got fired a couple of years ago, he'd never in his life held any job but police officer in this town. I don't have to tell you what kind of pay he was getting. His wife—her name's Celeste—"

"I met her today," Shigata interrupted.

"Oh?"

"Well, saw her, anyway. Hansen and I were over at Jack Horan's place. She came in, made a face like a gargoyle, and left again. Hansen told me who she was."

Quinn nodded. "She probably saw your car and decided to check out rumors. Anyhow, her and Shipp've been married about seventeen years—and she never has held a job outside her home. They say she's plenty thrifty, and I guess she'd have to be. Because he owns that house, a two-year-old Pontiac, a two-year-old crew-cab pickup truck, and a fourteen-foot speedboat and motor. Besides K and S. And I've heard he doesn't owe a cent on any of it. I suppose not having kids helps, but still—" He left the sentence elaborately unfinished.

"I hear you," Shigata said. He swung the car door open.

"Any special way to play it?" Quinn asked on the sidewalk.

"By ear," Shigata said.

Dale Shipp opened the front door himself, his expression souring when he saw who was standing there. He forced his

114

features into a grotesque semblance of a smile. "Celeste told me you'd picked up Hansen," he said. "Good work."

"It was pretty easy to do," Shigata said. "He came right into the office."

"What would he do a stupid thing like that for?"

"He was looking for you."

"Yeah," Quinn said, "looking for you. You know he's got a new lawyer, don't you, Shipp?"

"A new lawyer?"

"That's right," Shigata said. "We've been over the evidence. Galveston County gave it back to us a couple of months ago. It looks to me like you missed a couple of things in the investigation. 'Course, I can understand that, upset as you must have been. But I figure he's going to walk."

"Going to—"

"I'll be putting him back on the department, of course. Same rank as when he left. We're reworking the case."

"Reworking—"

"You sound like a fuckin' broken record, Shipp," Quinn said roughly. "Yeah. We're reworking the case. Hansen no more killed his wife and daughter—'scuse me, *your* daughter—than me or Shigata did."

"So who—"

"We're not quite ready to make a case," Shigata said. "That's why I stuck everything in the safe overnight. We're going back through it all tomorrow. But I figure once we're ready to make a case we'll hold off on it until we've got Hansen back on the street. I'd like to let him make the bust himself. He deserves that much, after what all he's been through. Wouldn't you say so, Shipp?"

Shipp swallowed. "You need any help from me?" he asked.

"Yeah, I could stand for you to come in maybe tomorrow afternoon and make a new statement. I'll take it myself. Some of your reports seem to have, uh, gotten lost. Courts, you know, they will lose things. I understand you were the one who found it all?"

"No," Shipp said, "no, that was that kid, the boy, Ted, Todd, Tim, ever what his name was. He found it and went tearing over next door and the neighbor, a fellow named, oh, what was his name, Miller I think it was, called me."

"Thanks for the clarification. I understand you called Galveston to help with the crime scene?"

"Uh, yeah."

"Who came up? Massey? Gentry? Conroe?"

"Gentry and Conroe. I never could understand why Galveston wants a woman to do a job like that. Too complicated and dirty for a woman."

"Right," Quinn said genially. "We only want women to do nice clean jobs like changing diapers and cleaning up puke. And simple jobs like teaching a class full of thirty kids to read and write."

"Quinn, what are you doing here anyway?" Shipp asked. "You're not a detective. What makes you think you're involved in this? Solving murders is a little tougher than handing out parking tickets."

"Right," Quinn said. "Shigata, did I ever tell you about that suicide Shipp worked while I was in oil-field security?"

"No, I don't guess you did."

"Fellow shot himself in the back with a bolt-action rifle. Five times at that. And then damned if he didn't swallow the gun. Newspapers just loved it. And then there was the taxicab driver who went out to meet the train—"

"Shut up, Quinn," Shipp said.

"Head on," Quinn added with a beatific smile. "Shigata, I guess I'm ready to go home now. Let me know when Shipp's going to come in and make a statement. I'll help you."

"I'm sure you'll be a lot of help. How about it, Shipp? Quinn and I are both dead on our feet. I probably won't get back up there till about noon."

"Uh, maybe two o' clock okay?"

"Sounds fine," Shigata said. "I'll be looking for you."

In the car, Quinn asked, "What time are you really getting up there?"

"I told Hansen I'd pick him up at seven-thirty. Right after that. And I'm going to have Ames sitting in the office all night with a shotgun. I don't know whether Shipp'll try for

116

the safe in the dark or in the daylight. Get some sleep, Al."

"Are you really going to leave the stuff in the safe?"

"Oh, hell, no," Shigata said. "I'm taking it home with me."

"What if he doesn't fall for it?"

"If he doesn't fall for it, he'll be coming after me."

"That," Quinn said, "is what I'm afraid of."

"I'll put on a bulletproof vest."

"He shoots people in the head, or hadn't you noticed?"

"I've noticed," Shigata said. "He also shoots at point-blank range. And I'm not getting that close to him."

"You were that close to him ten minutes ago."

"I had you with me. He couldn't take us both at once, and if he tried to take us in succession the other one would get him."

"Right," Quinn said, climbing out of the car. Then he stuck his head back in. "Okay. I know I can't stay with you all the time. But if I were you, I'd get Melissa and Gail out of the house and have them spend the night in a motel."

"I may do that."

"Call me if you get Shipp before noon. Otherwise, I'll be up there about one or so. If I don't hear from you, I'll be seeing what I can salvage of the garden in the morning."

"Right," Shigata said. "See you tomorrow."

The house, as usual, was full of kids, ranging in age from just over a year to late teens. Two or three of them were gone; Quinn was so tired he'd have had to call the roll to figure out exactly which ones were gone.

Nguyen looked at him. "You decide yet?"

He shook his head. "I'm trying to figure it out, Nguyen. I haven't put it out of my mind. But we've got a lot of trouble at the police station right now."

"That man Hansen?"

He nodded.

"Al, I tell you then he di'n' do it."

"I know you did. And you were probably right. That doesn't mean we can convince a jury of it."

"Juries stupid."

117

"Baby, you got that in one."

"You wan' supper?"

"Uh-uh. I just want to go to bed."

"You go. Kids! Television off now. You be quiet."

Quinn made his way through the assorted kids to the bedroom. He shut the door, opened the door, evicted a couple of cats and one of his children, shut the door again, and turned on the fan to drown out the noise, which would be continuing for at least an hour, of Nguyen periodically shushing kids who would shush for about two minutes and then resume giggling, talking, fighting, or crying.

Shigata was right about one thing, he thought. *I can't work deep nights for long. Not unless I sleep in the locker room.*

Shigata drove about two blocks and then reached for his hand mike. "Car one to Ames."

"Ames, go ahead."

"Can you meet me in the Winn-Dixie parking lot?"

"Ten-four. Be about five."

Shigata drove into the Winn-Dixie parking lot and waited on the corner by the fast-photo kiosk. The arriving patrol car nosed in beside him, facing the opposite direction, so that the drivers' windows were facing one another.

"I didn't want to put this on the air," Shigata said. "I want you to go directly into the station, park your car, and meet me inside. I've got a stakeout for you."

"You don't want me to go directly to the stakeout?"

"It's in my office," Shigata said.

"In your—"

"I think somebody's going to try for my safe tonight. The person it'll be knows the combination and probably has all the keys to the station."

The keys were all marked "Do Not Copy," and Shipp had supposedly turned in the keys he was issued. That, Shigata was aware, did not necessarily mean the keys had not been copied and did not necessarily mean Shipp had turned them in.

With Ames following him, Shigata drove toward the police station.

118

He worried all the way. They'd been heavy-handed talking to Shipp, partly because Quinn didn't really know how to play good cop-bad cop, partly because Shigata didn't want to be too subtle and risk not being understood. Shipp knew they had him tagged, Shigata was sure of that, but would Shipp be more likely to go after the evidence, which had remained securely in Galveston for three and a half years, or would he be more likely to go after Shigata?

He couldn't go after Hansen. Hansen was safe . . . but would he go after the jail, thinking Hansen was there?

Have I set something in motion that I can't control? Have I started a juggernaut moving?

What reason would Shipp have for wanting to kill Shelley Morgan? Hansen seems to feel she truly loved her sister, so she wouldn't be helping Shipp to cover up that murder. What else?

She's an accountant.

Shipp is living a lot higher than his income could support.

The IRS pays people who turn in tax evaders.

Am I onto something? Or am I just too tired to think straight?

He took the collection from the sand butt into the office and set it on his desk, and methodically sorted through it, periodically tossing away pebbles, small shells, and assorted cat coprolites. What was left was a small pile of lead. It would add up to about a hundred wadcutters.

There was not one copper-jacketed slug in the pile.

Not that he had expected to find one.

He began to make out lab sheets. He didn't have to worry about the casts of the tire tracks or the tires from Shelley's car; Truax would take care of them. But the slugs. The slugs.

(1) Determine whether all the plain lead slugs were fired from the same pistol. (2) Determine whether any of the plain lead slugs were fired from either of the two pistols enclosed, makes and serial numbers as shown. If so, please tell which slugs came from which pistols. (3) Determine whether any of the copper-jacketed slugs came from either of these two pistols. If so which slugs

119

came from which pistol? (4) Determine whether previously examined questioned slugs and previously examined exemplar slug came from either of the enclosed pistols. (5) Determine whether questioned slug "4" was fired from either of these pistols. (6) Determine whether questioned slug "4" was fired from the same pistol as previously examined questioned and exemplar slugs. (7) If none of the copper-jacketed slugs was fired from either of these pistols, please determine what type of pistol fired the copper-jacketed slugs.

It was, he judged, enough to keep a firearms examiner busy most of the week. Which made it unfortunate that he wanted the answers at once.

The guns— *Oh hell. I gave the .357 back to Hansen. Well, I'll get it in the morning.*

Melissa was asleep on the couch, her white gown and silver-blond hair making her look as delicate and fragile as the gossamer angel atop a Christmas tree. He didn't want to wake her, but he had to.

"You know Dale Shipp?" he asked her.

She paled slightly. "Yes. I know him."

"Then you won't ask why on this. Wake Gail up and both of you go to the Holiday Inn in Galveston. Call me when you get there."

"You're staying here?"

"Yes. But not where he'd be likely to look for me."

"I don't want to go, Mark."

"I know you don't. I don't want you to. I'd rather you just sit up with me. But if we both stay here, Gail stays here too. I don't really think he'll come here, and if he does he'll most likely come with a pistol. But there's always the outside chance he'll use a Molotov cocktail, a firebomb. The fewer people I have to worry about, the easier I can get myself out."

He woke, cramped from sleeping on the hall floor, to a very early dawn. *If he were going to come here, he'd certainly have done it during the night. He wouldn't have waited till daylight. So he's not coming here. And he didn't go to the office, because if he had done so Ames would have called me.*

Maybe he didn't fall for it. Damn it. If he doesn't, what next?

What next?

He called Melissa to let her know he was okay. "But I think you and Gail better stay in Galveston at least another day."

"What about Gail's school?"

"She misses school today. Obviously. Does he know you by sight? Shipp, I mean?"

"Yes." A tight voice. No explanation. That tone of voice that told Shigata not to ask for an explanation.

"Then you'd better stay indoors. Use room service and watch TV. I'm sorry, I know it's inconvenient, but—"

"I'm just worried about you."

"I'll be okay. Al won't let me get into too much trouble."

A little ripple of laughter. "No. He won't. And Nguyen won't let *him* get in too much trouble."

"Right."

A shower. Clean clothes. He'd wait for breakfast until after he'd picked up Hansen, because Hansen would be hungry too.

Seven-thirty. I told him I'd pick him up about now. He should be awake.

But there was no answer to Shigata's knock on the door. He knocked a second time, louder, and still got no response. *Maybe he's in the shower.*

Maybe he's not in the shower. What the hell did I let him have a pistol for, knowing he was at least halfway suicidal? Come on, Hansen, open the door.

Hansen did not open the door. Quite calmly, Shigata walked to the office, showed his badge, and asked for the passkey.

Hansen was lying on his back, chest bare, the sheet up to his waist. The slow rise and fall of his chest was reassuring. But his head was turned slightly to the side, and he hadn't even noticed the door opening, or Shigata moving around

121

the room. He was sleeping as heavily as if he'd been drugged. *What would he have taken? Where the hell would he have gotten anything?*

Shigata put his hand on Hansen's shoulder and shook him. "Wake up, Hansen."

"Umm-hmm." Hansen turned over on his side, shook off the hand, and went on sleeping.

"Hey, buddy, it's seven-thirty."

"Uh-huh." He flopped over on his stomach, head again turned to the side, and went on sleeping.

One long blond hair lay across the pillow beside him. *How in the hell did he get a woman in here? Well, that explains why he doesn't want to wake up. I wouldn't either, if I'd been locked away from it three and a half years and finally got some again. Only she's not here now. Whoever she is. Unless she's in the bathroom, and I don't think she is because the bathroom door is open.*

Well, he's not going to wake up now. Oh, I could make him get up, but why bother? I'll just get the pistol and leave—come back later for him—

The gunbelt lay on the small table beside the window. It was completely stocked, including a can of Mace Shigata didn't recall seeing the day before. Fully stocked including a regulation Smith & Wesson, K frame, four-inch barrel, with a piece of blue embossed tape on the gun butt that read "Barndt."

"Well, well, well," Shigata said under his breath. "So that's it."

He approached the bed, shook Hansen again. "Hansen, you hear me?"

"Uh-huh." A little more response, still not much.

"I'm taking your pistol on in for the Ranger. Call me when you're ready to get up. I'll come back and get you."

" 'Kay."

I hope he remembers.

Shigata didn't take just the pistol. He took the entire gunbelt. In the car, he said, "Car one to car fourteen. You on the road?"

"Yes, sir." Barndt's voice.

"Meet me at the Winn-Dixie parking lot."

"Ten-four."

She was there before he was. He rolled his window down, held the gunbelt out, and said, "Swap you."

Her face scarlet, she silently accepted her own gunbelt and took off and handed over Hansen's.

"You must have dressed in the dark," Shigata said.

"I did."

"Well, if it makes you feel any better, he's still asleep. He won't know you made the switch."

"Good. Don't tell him, okay?"

"I try my best not to get involved with my officers' private lives, unless it's something that looks likely to affect their work. I'd just hate for either of you to get hurt."

"He won't," Claire said. "If I do, that's the breaks. It won't affect my work."

"That's a load of crap," Shigata said, "but it's your business."

"Chief," Barndt said.

Shigata took his foot back off the gas pedal. "What?"

"You know what he told me?"

"No, what?"

"He told me he'd been thinking about it and he wanted me to lock him back up. So that if something else happened he'd have an alibi."

"What did you tell him?"

"I said I would. Only, then he went to sleep and so I just left. Nothing's happened all night, but I kept thinking, what if something did? And I hadn't brought him in?"

"He's got a point," Shigata said. "I'll talk with him about it later."

"Okay."

My subconscious is trying to tell me something, and I can't think what it is. Something about pistols. Something about switching pistols. Let's see, Hansen said right then he was working in uniform so he was using the long-barreled pistol. He said he used the short one when he was working plain-clothes. He said whichever pistol he wasn't using he kept locked up.

Where?

Where did he keep it locked up?

At home? Would Lillian have gotten it out to try to defend herself? Or Gaylene, considering she did know how to shoot?

At the police station? Where Shipp could get it? Because I don't for one second believe there was anything there he couldn't get his hands on, including men's private lockers.

I'm satisfied that Hansen didn't kill anybody. I'm convinced in my own mind that Shipp did it. But if Shipp used either of Hansen's pistols and I send them to the lab, I might as well take out a pistol and kill Hansen myself, because the result is going to be the same.

I know the .357 wasn't used, because I know it has six lands and grooves and a right-hand twist, and the copper jackets have five lands and grooves and a right-hand twist. But I don't know the land-and-groove pattern of a Colt.

I'm convinced Shipp did it. But what if he used the Colt to do it?

If I don't send the pistols to the lab, we never will know the answer.

Ames wasn't asleep. He looked up, pistol in hand, when Shigata opened the door. Then he lowered the pistol and started to stand up.

"Nothing?" Shigata asked.

Ames shook his head. "Nothing."

"Well, that's the breaks. Thanks for trying. Go write yourself down for overtime."

"Is this about Hansen?" Ames asked.

"What makes you ask that?"

"The radio says we've got him. And he's damn sure not in jail."

"What do you know about Hansen?"

"This is a small town, chief. I've lived in it all my life. I'm three years older than his daughter, but I knew her. Dated her once, in fact. And Hansen came to talk to my scout troop a few times when I was a kid."

"What do you think about him?"

124

"I think he was set up. Everybody in town thinks that. If they'd tried him here instead of in Galveston, they couldn't have found enough people who didn't think that to make up a jury. But of course, Galveston's the county seat."

"True. Yes, this was about Hansen."

"Trying to catch him, or trying to clear him?"

"Trying to clear him."

"Then I don't want any overtime pay." Ames headed for the locker room.

Hansen didn't know that. Hansen honestly thought everybody in town had turned against him. Means somebody bought his lawyer. Who? And why?

Do the motives for this run deeper than we thought?

Shigata laid the box of evidence on his desk, took out the gunbelt he'd dropped in it, drew the pistol, and taped a red notice to it: *"Warning! Loaded Gun!"* He added a similar sign to the other pistol, sealed both pistols in plastic bags, and put the bags in the box. Then he added the box of ammunition Shipp had left in the desk. He'd add a note later asking the lab to see if the copper-jacketed slugs—the fatal ones—had come from this box. He set the evidence box on the floor. It would be ready for Truax, whenever Truax showed up.

The telephone rang. "Shigata?" said a rather apologetic voice on the other end. "Did you try to wake me up?"

"Yes. You didn't seem too eager to greet the day."

"Did you get my gunbelt?"

"Yeah, to send the .357 to Austin. I figured I'd just let you go on and sleep."

"I'm sorry. Why don't I just walk over there, seeing as it's not but a couple of blocks?"

Shigata hesitated, then said, "I guess so."

Hansen was within sight of the police station when a car stopped beside him. "Going anywhere?" asked a hideously familiar voice.

"No, Shipp," he said, "I'm not going anywhere at all."

"Hands on top of your head, boy."

125

Hansen put his hands on top of his head and waited for Shipp to walk around and unlock the passenger's door. And then he kicked backward, like a mule, as hard as he could kick.

� placeholder for triangle symbol

Chapter 9

TRUAX GRABBED FOR HIS mike. "Backups in front of the Bayport Police Station. Shots fired." Then he slammed the emergency brake into position and catapulted out of the white Plymouth. By now he'd heard at least two bursts of gunfire, and Hansen and Shipp were slugging it out on the street. A lot of blood from somewhere had spilled on the asphalt, and Truax saw Hansen slip in it.

Hansen half fell and caught himself, and the two men broke apart. A third shot rang out, the slug singing over Truax's head and ricocheting off a brick wall somewhere behind him. Instinctively he ducked and then resumed running, drawing as he ran. No matter who had started out with the gun, Shipp definitely had it now, and he didn't seem to care who was behind Hansen and likely to get hit. Hansen slipped in the blood again. This time he landed on the ground on his back.

But he continued to stay just outside of Shipp's reach by methodically kicking, alternately at Shipp's gun hand and his legs, until he managed to pull Shipp off balance. Shipp went down on top of Hansen, slugging at his face and trying to get the pistol back into firing position.

Hansen succeeded in rolling over, so that he was now on top of Shipp. That made it fairly easy for Truax to grab him and drag him off.

"This escapee pulled a gun—" Shipp began, scrambling to his feet with the pistol still in his hand.

"It's Shipp's gun," Hansen said, somewhat more calmly. "Truax, you know what I'm doing here."

The blood did appear to be coming from Hansen, not Shipp, and the gun—a perfectly ordinary Smith & Wesson service revolver, blue steel with a four-inch barrel—seemed to have some relationship to Shipp's hand-tooled leather hip holster.

By this time Shigata was out of the police station heading toward them, pistol in hand, and another Bayport police car had turned the corner, siren screaming.

Shipp looked around. Looked at Shigata, looked at Hansen, looked at Truax. Wiped a smear of blood from his face—apparently Hansen's blood, as there was no cut under it. And then, moving as fast as an eel, he was into his pickup truck. He backed, turned, slammed hard into the right front fender of the police car, and kept going. "Son of a bitch!" Truax shouted. Literally dropping Hansen, he ran for the Plymouth. After a quick U-turn, he took off after Shipp.

Hansen, suddenly free of restraint, staggered a little and sat down hard on the street. He was back on his feet, clutching his left side, before Shigata and the driver of the disabled patrol car could reach him. There seemed to be quite a lot of blood oozing between his fingers. "Never mind me," he panted, "get the slug. Shigata, get the slug, get the *slug*!"

"We'll get the slugs," Shigata said, "but let me have a look at you now."

"It just skinned my ribs, I'm okay—Shigata—he knows where Todd is. He knows—"

"Truax is on top of him. Why would he want to go after Todd?"

"Truax hasn't stopped him. He won't be able to. I know what Shipp does to his engines. He'd go after Todd to stop me."

It was obviously true that Truax hadn't stopped him yet;

his siren, though fainter, was still audible in the distance.

"You sure that's just a skinned rib?" *I don't think he's going after Todd. But I won't get any more sense out of Hansen until he's sure Todd is safe. Not that I can blame him for that.*

What I want to know is, why the hell did Shipp flip out like that?

"Positive. That kind of thing bleeds like crazy, you know that."

"Probably doesn't feel too great, either," Shigata said. "You need a doctor."

"Todd first. Then the slugs. Then the doctor."

"All right, come on, we'll go get Todd. Phillips!" he shouted to the patrol officer. "Keep people away. I'll have Quinn up here in a minute."

Hansen, climbing into the Bronco, said, "I'm going to bleed all over your car."

"Never mind the car." Shigata grabbed for the radio. "Car one to headquarters, call Quinn and get him up there. Have him twenty-nine Phillips on Main Street in front of the PD. Tell him he's got to find some slugs in the street."

"Slugs?"

"Expended bullets," Shigata said patiently, driving toward Shelley Morgan's house. "Don't worry, Quinn will understand."

"Yes, sir. How many?"

"Stand by. How many shots were fired?" he asked Hansen.

"I don't know. Two or three. Maybe four. I think it was three."

"Headquarters, there should be at least two slugs, more likely three, possibly four."

"Ten-four, I've got Quinn on the phone."

"Ten-four, I'm switching over to state radio. Monitor city and state both. Truax, you copy?"

"I copy." Shigata and Hansen could hear the siren wailing behind the radio as Truax spoke.

"You still on him?"

"Ten-four, and I've got county and highway patrol units

coming, but that fu—that truck must have a rocket engine."

"Ten-four, do your best to stay on him. Bayport dispatch, you copy?"

"Yes, sir, and Quinn's en route."

"Tell him I need those slugs more than I need him on this chase."

"Ten-four."

"Truax, you still on him?"

"Ten-four, I'm out on Bayshore Drive headed for I-45. Sheriff's units en route up 45 from Galveston."

"Highway patrol unit southbound on 45," said an unidentifiable voice from the radio. "What am I looking for?"

"Yellow Ford crew-cab, white male driver," Truax said. Going like a bat out of Hades. *Shit!*" Metal crashed, and then the radio went silent.

"What happened, Truax?" Shigata asked sharply.

"He shot out my left front tire. I'm in a ditch by that concrete balk on the Bayshore on ramp. He's doubled back, looks like he's going back into town. Where's that highway patrol unit?"

"Still eight miles north of Bayport, going south on I-45," said the unfamiliar voice.

"Ten-four, I'll be commandeering your vehicle."

"Ten-four, let me clear it with my station."

Shigata switched back to city radio. "Phillips, is your car drivable?"

"That's affirmative."

"You know where Dale Shipp lives?"

"Yes, sir."

"Get over there. If he shows up, stop him. Use whatever force it takes. Consider him armed and very dangerous."

"Ten-four. En route."

As Shigata rounded the curve near Shelley's house, Quinn's voice came over the radio. "I've found the location of the incident. Who was hurt?"

Shigata grabbed the mike. "Your—uh—former drinking buddy."

"Ten-four. How bad?"

Hansen took the mike. "Not bad. Skinned ribs is all."

"Who was where?"

"We were grappling. Both of us were all over the ground. I've got powder burns, so at least one shot was real close. But I couldn't tell you the directions."

Truax cut in. "I heard one of 'em hit a wall. I think it was by the library."

"Ten-four. I'll look for the slugs."

"Look till you find them," Shigata said. "Headquarters, car one is ten-six."

There was no car at Shelley's house, and every door and window stood open. Hansen went in the door at a dead run. "Todd!" he shouted.

Todd was sitting on a turquoise imitation-Naugahyde couch watching TV and eating potato chips. Except that he was now wearing blue jeans, a sweat shirt, and sneakers without socks, he might not have moved since Saturday morning. He turned his head languidly, not quite far enough to see either Hansen or Shigata, and said, "Huh?"

"Where's Marion?" Hansen demanded.

"She went home. She'll be back tomorrow."

"And left you here alone?"

"I told her I was going to stay with a friend."

"Then why aren't you at your friend's house?"

"Because I didn't want to go."

"Didn't you spare a thought for safety?"

"I'm safe. Long as you're not around."

"If they gave an Academy Award for stupid, you'd be the hands-down winner!" Hansen shouted. "Kid, can't you get it through your head—"

"Never mind that now," Shigata interrupted. "Todd, lock up. You're coming with us."

"Why?" He reached for another handful of potato chips. He still hadn't looked at either of them.

"Because I damn well said so," Hansen shouted, and grabbed Todd by the shoulder from behind.

Todd jerked away, came to his feet, and—finally—turned. His eyes widened. "What happened to you?"

"I got shot," Hansen said. At Todd's stricken look, he added, "It's not bad. I'll be okay. Just grab whatever you need for a couple of days and come on. We're getting out of here."

"Who shot you?" Todd asked, making no move to get anything.

"Dale Shipp."

"Gaylene's fa—?"

"Yes, Gaylene's father. Todd, never mind that, just come on—you can get clothes later—" He was propelling Todd toward the door as he spoke.

"Doesn't it hurt?"

"You're as hard to move as a Missouri mule! Hell, yes, it hurts. Now, come on."

"Then why didn't you go to a doctor?"

"I'll go to a doctor later. Right now, getting you where Shipp can't find you is far more important." He glanced around. Shigata was moving quietly through the house, shutting doors and windows.

"Why?" Todd asked, stopping again at the door from the kitchen to the carport.

"Because, as unlikely as this may seem to you, as hard as it may be for you to believe, I love you." By now he had succeeded in propelling Todd out the door, and Shigata followed.

"Hey, I haven't got my key!" Todd protested.

"Tough shit," Shigata told him, closing the kitchen door. "We gave you time to grab stuff and you wanted to stand around and argue instead."

"Yeah, but—"

"Yeah but what?" Hansen said. "Fasten your seat belt."

Todd located and fastened his seat belt. "Dad," he asked, "why?"

"Why what? Get your hand out of the way, I'm closing this door."

As Hansen climbed, with increasing awkwardness, into the front seat of the Bronco, Todd asked, "Why do you love me? I think if I had a kid that treated me like I've been treating you, I'd get pretty tired of it."

"Then you're lucky I'm not you. Anyway, I didn't say I wasn't pretty tired of it. I didn't say I wasn't mad at you. Frankly, I could wring your cotton-picking neck about now, and if I catch you eating another potato chip for the next six months I may just do it. I didn't raise you to be a couch potato. But I didn't stop loving you because I got mad at you."

"Was it him that killed Mom and Gaylene? And Shelley? Was it Dale Shipp that did that?"

"It's about a hundred percent certain on Lillian and Gaylene," Hansen said, "but we don't know for sure about Shelley. I don't know why he would've done it, but we can't think who else might have had a reason either. Shigata, where are we going to take Todd?"

"Over to Quinn's. That's what we usually do with kids until we can take them where they belong. Nguyen never minds."

"Nguyen wouldn't. But will it be safe? I mean, if he realizes that's where we would take him—with all those kids over there— What I'm saying is, I want to keep Todd safe, but not by risking somebody else's safety."

"If Hoa's in port, we could ask him to take Todd out on the boat. Damn sure thing nobody'll get at him there."

"Who's Hoa?"

"Quinn's brother-in-law, Nguyen's brother. Runs a shrimp boat out of Galveston."

"Why can't I stay with you?" Todd demanded from the back seat.

"Because there'll probably be more shooting," Hansen said.

"Then you shouldn't be there either."

"Very reasonable suggestion. But I've got to—"

"Anyway, there's something I have to tell you, and it's very important."

Shigata pulled the car over on the side of the road. "There's not much use driving until I know where I'm driving to," he said.

"Okay, Todd, what is it you need to tell me?" Hansen asked, turning so that he could look into the back seat.

133

"That night, when all that happened, you were right, where you guessed I was."

"Okay. I figured that."

"And just as I was coming home, I saw Mr. Shipp leaving. I didn't think anything about it, I just thought he'd been over to see Gaylene, but it was funny because it was real late at night and he didn't have his headlights on. And by the next morning I forgot about it. I completely forgot. I don't know how I could—"

"Grief and shock make us forget things," Hansen said. "So do drugs. You'd mixed codeine and marijuana."

"If I had remembered that then, would it have helped you?"

"Possibly," Hansen said. "It's hard to say for sure. Don't worry about it now. You can't undo the past."

"It definitely helps now," Shigata said.

"Car two to car one."

"Go ahead," Shigata said.

"I've got two slugs, " Quinn said. "Is that going to be enough?"

"How good a shape are they in?"

"The one that hit the library's in pretty bad shape. The other's okay. Tell Han—tell my drinking buddy he's got a chip out of a rib."

"Tell him I'm not surprised," Hansen said.

"He says he's not surprised. Yeah, that ought to do it."

"They're both copper jackets."

"Ten-four."

"Okay, I'm going to go see if I can help that trooper get Truax out of the ditch. Is all that stuff on your desk ready to go?"

"Stand by," Shigata said. "Hansen, that includes both your pistols. Is there any chance at all Shipp used your snub-nose? Because if there is, I don't want to risk—"

"He didn't. It was where he couldn't get at it. If he used anything of mine, it was the Dan Wesson."

"He didn't use it," Shigata said positively. "I had a case before involving a Dan Wesson. It has six lands and grooves and a right-hand twist. A Smith & Wesson—just about any Smith & Wesson, so far as I know—has five lands and grooves and a right-hand twist. So do the slugs from your house, and the one from the field. But I don't know what a Colt has because I don't use a Colt and I've never had a case where I needed to know about one. The lead in your sand butt—all of it has six lands and grooves. I couldn't tell the twist on all of it."

"What did you do, go back out there and dig it up last night?"

"Yep, me and Quinn. Quinn and I."

"You've been hanging around South Texas too long. You're starting to talk like us. Yeah, I told you I practiced with both pistols. But the snub-nose was locked up that night in a case in the trunk of my car. So there was no way Shipp could get at it."

"Okay." Shigata picked up the mike again. "Car one to car two. It's all ready to go."

"Ten-four. I'll turn it over to Truax."

"Ten-four," Shigata said.

"Mr.—um—Shigata," Todd said from the back seat.

"Yeah?"

"Does that mean they could have proved right then my dad didn't do it?"

"Yes, if he'd had a defense attorney with any brains in his head, so the right questions got asked."

"An attorney worth his salt?" Todd asked.

"You could put it that way."

"Oh," Todd said. "Well, I wish I'd known that."

"I wish you had too," Hansen said, wriggling in his seat belt. "Speaking of salt—"

"What?" Shigata asked.

"You ever get gunpowder in a cut?"

"Yeah. It's one of those things if you ever did it once you never want to do it again. You ought to have bled enough to wash it out."

"Apparently I haven't. Damn that hurts—damn, damn, damn, I think I'm rubbing more in with this shirt."

"Dad, you've got to go to a doctor," Todd said from the back seat.

"Forget it," Hansen answered. "First we get Shipp. Then I go to the doctor. Shigata, can you pull into that drugstore up there?"

"Okay," Shigata said.

Hansen got a twenty out of his pocket and handed it to Todd. "You go in there and buy a lot of gauze and a lot of tape and a bottle of peroxide. Got it?"

"Yes, sir."

As he vanished into the store, Hansen asked, "You know about the four stages of grief?"

"I don't think so," Shigata said.

"First is disbelief. This can't be happening. It isn't true. Then anger. Anger at whoever's around to be angry at, even anger at the person who's dead for dying. Then bargaining. A feeling that if I do this or I do that then things will be back like they were. Or if I had done this or that then it wouldn't have happened—guilt, as well as bargaining. Finally, acceptance. Todd's been stuck on the anger stage. I don't think he ever really believed I did it. But he was suddenly, horribly, abandoned by both parents and his sister. I was the only one alive for him to be mad at. So he was hating me for being alive and for having abandoned him—no matter how unwillingly I abandoned him—and at the same time he hated himself for hating me, because in one part of his mind he knew none of it was my doing. Now he's trying to bargain—if he had told this, if he had done that—he's going to come up with two or three dozen 'if only's' before it's over. It's never completely straightforward, he'll be back into anger again and again before it's over, but that's just the way it is. That didn't take long," he said as Todd scrambled back into the back seat.

"Where do we go for this?" Shigata asked.

"My motel room is closest. If I just knew—if *we* just knew—where Shipp is. He can't know for sure where I stayed last night, but from where he saw me walking, he'll know it wasn't far. Does he have a key to this car?"

"No, this is the one major police department purchase so far that I made."

"Good. Then let's just go to the motel."

"You never did tell me what happened."

"When Shipp saw me? He made like he was arresting me. But I knew damn well if I got in the car with him that was that. I waited till he got behind me and then kicked him in the balls."

Shigata chuckled. "I expect he didn't like that."

"No. He didn't like that."

"Dad, how could he arrest you if he's not a cop anymore?"

"Citizen's arrest. Technically, I'm still an escapee."

"The TV said you were in custody."

"I am. Sort of. But I certainly wasn't visibly in custody walking down Main Street. . . . Okay." He unlocked the door, stepped inside, and stripped off his jacket, shirt, and undershirt. "Damn! He got me twice!"

"You'll be feeling that awhile," Shigata observed, setting his radio down on the table by the front window.

"No shit, Sherlock. Here, Todd, you want to do the honors?"

"Huh?"

"You want to clean this and get a bandage on me?"

"Clean it with peroxide?"

"That's what we bought it for."

"It'll hurt."

"It won't hurt *you*."

"You know what I mean."

"My son, my son," Hansen said, "if you want a place where nobody ever gets hurt, you aren't going to find it on this earth. You don't have to do this if you don't want to. It'll hurt me just as much whether you or Chief Shigata does it. Anyway, peroxide won't be near as bad as alcohol would be."

"Let him do it anyway."

"Okay," Shigata said, detaching himself from the chair he'd briefly sat down on. "Hansen, let's get you in here where I've got some water. Todd, can you bring the chair so your dad can sit down beside this sink? Okay—this one isn't deep."

137

"I know," Hansen said, craning his neck to get a better look at the cuts. "That one really did just skin my ribs. But that's the one—ouch—that the gunpowder got in."

"The gunpowder got in both of them. You've got powder burns all over your shirttail. I think this is the cracked rib."

"I think so too. Take it easy with that tape." Hansen's voice was tightly controlled.

"Dad," Todd said, "if I hadn't sneaked off that night, maybe none of it would have happened."

"And if I hadn't gone and spent the night on the beach, maybe it wouldn't have happened. Which is somewhat more likely. There's a poem I learned when I was a lot younger than you are now. I want you to learn it."

"Your voice sounds funny. I mean, not funny."

"Right," Hansen said, and managed a quick grin at Shigata, who did not grin back. "Now, here's the poem. It was written a long time ago in Persia—that's what is now called Iran—and translated about, oh, sixty-odd years ago by a man in England.

> *The moving finger writes; and having writ,*
> *Moves on: nor all your piety nor wit*
> *Shall lure it back to cancel half a line,*
> *Nor all your tears wash out a word of it.*

Can you remember that?"

"What does it mean?"

"It means what happened, happened. We can't go back and change the past. The best we can do—*all* we can do—is pick up where we are and do the best with what we've got now."

Shigata turned to wash his hands, and Hansen stood up. "Thanks," he said.

"Okay."

Hansen reached for a clean shirt.

"Dad," Todd said, "there's something I don't understand."

"What's that, son?"

"How do you just keep on going? I mean, with all that's

138

happened to you, and me acting like I was acting, and everything—how do you just keep on going? I mean, it just seems like you'd get to the point where all you would want to do is sit in a corner and cry or something."

"I have done my full share and then some of sitting in a corner crying," Hansen replied. "But sitting in a corner crying doesn't solve any problems." His voice sounded muffled momentarily, as he pulled a T-shirt over his head. "It makes you feel a little better, that's all. So then you get up and get back to work on the problems. Yipe. Somebody help me get this shirt untangled . . . Thanks, Todd. Shigata, I don't know about you, but I'm hungry."

"Dad, if you—I mean if I don't remember everything at once, is that okay?"

"Of course it's okay."

"Because I just now remembered when you left that night and I didn't remember before. I was asleep, but not quite. Does that made sense?"

Hansen nodded, and Todd went on. "I remember you and Mom—you said something like 'Why can't you trust me?' and Mom started crying and said, 'I do trust you but you can't understand this' and you said 'I damn sure can't understand it if you don't tell me what it is you want me to understand' and Mom said 'Leave me alone, I need some time to breathe' and you said 'Okay, take some time to breathe, I'll talk to you in the morning,' and then you walked past me on the front porch and got in the car and left and Mom was crying and then she called somebody on the telephone."

"She called somebody on the telephone," Hansen repeated. "Do you know who?"

"No. But it seems like I ought to know. She called somebody on the telephone and then whoever she called came over, but I can't remember who it was and it feels like I ought to remember."

"Don't push it," Hansen said. "Don't try to remember. Let it go. You'll remember sometime."

"Yeah, but I need to remember now. I feel like I need to

remember now."

There was distress in his voice, and Hansen caught hold of him. "Don't worry at it, Todd. Let's go get some hamburgers, okay? Okay, Shigata?"

"If you're buying. I'm out of cash." *I'm also out of money, until payday. Taking a thirty-thousand-dollar-a-year pay cut when I changed jobs has put a decided crimp in my lifestyle.*

"I'm buying."

"But I'd rather we just get them and take them into the office," Shigata added. "I think you and I both need to stay as close to the radios as we can. And we've still got to figure out where Todd can go that's safe."

"Yeah," Hansen said.

"So the way I see it," Hansen said, "we can prove I didn't do it, but—"

"Not really," Shigata interrupted.

"What do you mean, 'not really'?"

"As you said yourself, we can't prove you didn't have another pistol, and we can't—so far—prove you didn't come back to the house that night after Todd left."

"Then what—"

"I can definitely prove that you had an unjust trial. That means we can definitely get you a new trial. And you'll be acquitted, because whether or not we can prove you're innocent, the state definitely cannot prove you're guilty. That's what we've got now. If we find out all those copper jackets were fired from the same pistol—which I think is going to happen—then at that point we can make a good strong case against Shipp, and prove you're innocent by proving somebody else guilty."

"Means I could sit in prison another two years while the legal wheels turn an inch at a time. And we still can't prove I didn't kill Shelley."

"There again, what we're going to have to do is prove that somebody else did. Don't worry about sitting in prison. I've got a lot of cards I haven't played. Todd."

"Yes, sir?" Todd, answering with sprigs of lettuce protruding from his mouth, bore a temporary resemblance to a feeding sea manatee.

"The person that came to the house after your mom called. Is there any possibility it was Shelley?"

"I don't think so. I think I would remember if it was Shelley."

"Okay. I've got to make a list of things I need to check on. This weekend has been so chaotic I keep remembering things I need to do and then forgetting them before I get a chance to do them or even write them down." He picked up a pen, and the telephone rang. "Like that," he said. "Hello?"

"I understand you have Steve Hansen in custody," said Jim Barlow in a less-than-friendly tone.

"Yes, why?"

"Where was he yesterday?"

"Yesterday when?"

"Yesterday when you were telling me you didn't know where he was."

"I haven't asked. Would you like to ask him yourself? Hold on. Hansen, I've got Jim Barlow on the phone. You want to talk to him?"

"Is he still SAC? Bureau?"

"Yes." Shigata could hear Barlow sputtering in the background.

"Yeah, I'll talk to him . . . Hello, Barlow. What was it you wanted to know about yesterday?"

"Where you were Sunday morning."

"My church attendance has been a little irregular lately."

"If you think this is some kind of joke—"

"I was holed up. And I'm not going to tell you where, because I might want to use the place again."

"And Saturday? Were you holed up Saturday?"

"Part of the day, yes. I spent some of the day in Galveston."

"Doing what?"

"Walking on the beach. Changing clothes."

"But Shigata didn't know where you were."

"No, sir, he did not."

"And Friday? He didn't know where you were Friday either?"

"No, sir."

"Then how in the hell did you get to Bayport?"

"I hitchhiked."

"You hitchhiked. You didn't get there until after business hours?"

"Barlow, you know damn well I was in court in Houston Friday till after four o'clock. What's this all about? If you're trying to imply Shigata helped me get away, you're a jackass. I got away because Rusty Claiborne was too stupid to fasten his seat belt, and so he knocked himself out on the windshield when he rolled the car. For cryin' out loud, Barlow, I never even *met* Shigata until after noon on Sunday."

"Then," Barlow said, "would you care to explain to me just exactly how it happens that Rusty Claiborne's possessions, to which you helped yourself, arrived back in Huntsville today by mail, having gone through a City of Bayport postage meter on Friday?"

"Is the Bureau reduced to working B and E's? I broke into the city offices Friday night and used the postage meter. But I left behind some money to pay for the postage, and I didn't do any damage when I broke in."

"Some of whose money?"

"My own," Hansen said. "My own. Whether you believe it or not. How's Claiborne?"

"What difference does it make to you?"

"He's been decent to me."

"He's okay," Barlow said grudgingly.

"Now let me ask you something," Hansen said. "You've known me for close to twelve years, right?"

"Something like that," Barlow admitted.

"Then why was it so damned easy for you to convict me of murder?"

"I didn't convict you. A court convicted you."

"Courts have been known to be wrong. But you didn't bother to look at any of the evidence."

"Give me the phone," Shigata said.

142

"Shigata wants the phone," Hansen said, and handed it over.

"Let me put it this way, Jim," Shigata said. "I have uncovered evidence that Hansen is innocent. I have also uncovered proof of very substantial civil-rights violations on the part of the Bayport Police Department while Dale Shipp was running it. My investigation is continuing. Would you like to become involved?"

"What kind of civil-rights violations?" Barlow asked, sounding somewhat less angry all of a sudden.

"I would consider a person who plotted to convict a defendant of two murders that other person knew he hadn't committed to be violating the defendant's civil rights," Shigata said.

"Mark, are you serious? This is not just because you like Hansen?"

"I was in Denver when Hansen went to prison," Shigata said, feeling like a broken record because he'd said all this so may times in the last two days. "The first time I saw him was after noon Sunday, when he walked into my office looking for Dale Shipp. Before that happened I was already investigating the evidence and coming to the conclusion that he had been set up, and that Dale Shipp did it to him and very likely committed the murders as well. Now, the murder investigation—I should say investigations, because there was a killing Saturday afternoon that is probably connected—are my department. You have no jurisdiction. But you have more jurisdiction than I do in the matter of civil-rights violations. I think we're also going to uncover proof of tax fraud, and that's your department entirely. I could use your help."

There was a long silence. Then Barlow said, "Shigata, if you're lying to me I'm going to break your neck. I'm in. What do you want me to do first?"

"We need two search warrants. Morgan's Accounting Services on Main Street, and Dale Shipp's house."

"What are we looking for and what's my probable cause?"

$\triangledown$

Chapter 10

SHIGATA'S OFFICE WASN'T LARGE enough. All of them—
Shigata, Quinn, Hansen, Todd Hansen, Jim Barlow, and two
more FBI agents—had moved to the large squad room between Shigata's office and the hall. Shigata, Quinn, and
Hansen had been confering over a list of things to do next;
now they were just sitting. Todd, tiring of sitting still, had
begun playing some complicated game that seemed to in-
volve kicking a small beanbag; everybody else except Barlow
was waiting. There wasn't anything else to do, not until
Barlow made his decisions.

Barlow read steadily through the files, which had been
augmented, during the two hours it took him to get the
search warrants and drive down from Houston, by reports
as complete as possible on Hansen's and Todd's memories
of the night of the killings, and Shigata's explanations of the
discrepancy in firearms and slugs. He stopped once, to ask,
"Where is Dale Shipp now?"

"Nobody's been able to locate him," Shigata answered.

"In a yellow crew-cab truck, he has managed to disappear?"

"So it would seem."

"I could understand if it were blue," Barlow said, "but
yellow—"

"This is Galveston County," Quinn reminded him.

"Why the hell did he take off like that, anyway?" Barlow demanded. "I mean, if you guys are right about what was going on, he'd been getting away with it for years. So why the sudden panic now?"

"I don't know," Shigata said. "I wish I did."

"He wasn't trying to arrest me," Hansen said softly. "He was trying to kill me. And Truax saw it. Up until then, all his ducks had been in a nice little row, but now—"

"Ducks are like dominoes," Quinn interrupted. "When they're all in a row, it's real easy to push them all over. Shigata and me, we went over to his house last night to try to rattle his cage. Looks like we rattled it real good."

Barlow looked at the faces around him. Then he said, "Let me read." When he finally laid the last piece of paper down, his face was ashen. "For this we sentenced a man to die?"

Todd stuck the beanbag—he called it a Hackiesack—into his pocket and drifted closer, obviously attempting to eavesdrop inconspicuously.

"It was twisted," Hansen said. "The jury didn't see what you're seeing. Neither did the prosecutor."

"And your attorney?"

"He was court-appointed. Young. Shigata thinks he might've been bought. I don't know. He might've just been inexperienced. If he made up his mind to start with that I was guilty, he might not have cared much about trying to defend me."

Barlow looked at Hansen. "You and I have had our differences," he said, "but this—" He shook the offending piece of paper angrily. "This is monstrous. Who did the crime scene?"

"Galveston," Hansen said.

"You haven't gotten statements from them yet?"

"That's one of the things on my list," Shigata said. "You wouldn't believe this weekend," he added. "And I have exactly two investigators. Counting Quinn and me."

"Do it now. You got a speakerphone?"

"Yes, but I don't like to use it."

"Right now we use it."

With everybody crowded back into his office—Todd, as the least official of the group, was standing in the doorway—Shigata dialed the number of the Galveston Police Department and asked for ident.

Donna Gentry answered. That was convenient. It saved the trouble of asking for her.

"Donna," Shigata said, "when you do a crime scene for a small neighboring town, like maybe us, do you keep records on it there? Or do you turn all records over to—"

"We keep them," Donna interrupted. "Why? You wondering about that Hansen case?"

"Yes," Shigata said. "How long would it take you to find them?"

"I've got them out already. I never did think he did it, you know, and I figured if he got to you you'd try to help him. Clear back before he went on trial I told his lawyer I wanted to testify for the defense, but he didn't call me, and the prosecution just asked what they wanted to ask. Like was I there and did I see the gun and did I take the pictures. And the defense didn't ask anything. I'd never seen such a stupid lawyer as Hansen had."

"Tell me why you don't think Hansen was guilty," Shigata said.

"How long have you got?"

"As long as it takes."

"Are you on a speakerphone? It sounds like you're down in a barrel."

"I'm on a speakerphone."

"Do you want to tell me who's on it with you?"

"No," Shigata said. "Let's just say it's nobody I mind hearing this discussion."

"Okay. Well, to start with, the gun that was supposed to have been used wasn't. Look, I'm no firearms expert, but even I could tell that. And Hansen's supposed to be some kind of genius. If he was setting something up to look like murder-suicide, which was what Shipp was insisting he'd done, he certainly wouldn't have made that sort of dumb mistake. Then we did trace metals on everybody except

146

Hansen: there was no use doing one on him because he'd definitely had the gun in his hand. The boy was completely clean. The girl had held a gun, but the position she was shot, she couldn't have shot herself. So somebody took the gun away from her, either before or after killing her. The adult victim had little traces—her left thumb and the first three fingers on her left hand had touched the gun metal—but you know how when somebody is really holding a gun their whole hand is just purple under the black light. Hers wasn't. She hadn't held a gun; she'd just had it touched to her hand, probably after she was dead. There were fingerprints on the gun, probably hers. I offered to lift 'em and print her for comparison, but Shipp said not to. Okay, there again, if it was somebody stupid, or somebody unfamiliar with firearms, I could understand that kind of mistake, but not Hansen."

"That's enough right there," Shigata said. "But what else do you have?"

"Well, the gunpowder residue. They sent copies to Bayport and copies to us, because we'd done the tests. Negative on the woman, the suspect, and the boy. Positive on the girl, but I already told you that."

"Shipp told Hansen they were inconclusive," Shigata said. "And the best I can tell, no report ever got to the DA."

"The hell they were inconclusive, Shigata, I've got the reports in my hand. They were *negative* except for the one on the girl. And when I told Shipp that, he said of course they were negative, Hansen had had plenty of time to wash his hands. I don't know exactly how he obfuscated the jury on that—of course, I was sequestered with the other witnesses—but whatever he said, it was a load of crap. He might could make a jury believe something like that, but he damn sure couldn't make me believe it. I offered to testify for Hansen last week when he was having that hearing—I wrote the judge and said I was certain there was a miscarriage of justice—and would you believe the judge's secretary called me and said they weren't looking at evidence, only at procedural errors! I mean, really! And I tried to write to Hansen himself, right after he was moved to Huntsville, and they sent my letter back and said I wasn't on the approved list of people for him to get mail from. Shigata, I've tried everything I could think of, I tried to talk to the DA, I tried to talk to the Grand Jury, and I couldn't get anybody to listen. When it happened I'd just made corporal and what does a corporal know? Are you trying to get something done about it? Because if you are, it's certainly about time. You can count me in."

"Donna, can you make me photocopies of your whole file and have somebody bring it up here?" Shigata said.

"Sure, when do you need it?"

"A week ago. But this afternoon'll do."

"I'll have it there in an hour," she said.

"Thanks," Shigata said. After the phone went silent, he turned to Hansen. "Now we know who fired your pistol. Gaylene."

Hansen nodded. "In a way I'm glad she tried to fight the son of a bitch," he said, "but to know she knew what was happening—I'd kind of hoped, the position she was in, that she was asleep and didn't know. . . . So I guess the finger-prints on the gun were Lillian's. Which is what I figured to start with."

"How do you figure that?" one of the young FBI agents demanded. "Couldn't they have been this Gaylene's?

Shigata, sounding weary, said, "The prints on the pistol were in suicide position. Gaylene held it in normal firing position. Lillian never held it at all. Somebody just touched it to her hand in suicide position."

"So somebody staged a suicide to make it look like Lillian did it," Quinn said. "Only, whoever did it was too dumb to realize different gun barrels mark the bullet different. Which doesn't sound like Shipp. He's stupid, but he ain't that stupid."

"It wasn't Shipp," Hansen said. "Whoever did it didn't know I don't use copper jackets. And Shipp does. That, he knows. But somebody set up a suicide. Then Shipp came in and he could see it wasn't a suicide. So it had to be murder. So it had to be me. Then, it had to be me. But within two

148

days, he knew it wasn't me. And after that his only concern was to make the frame fit real tight. Did I tell you he brought Bob Kerns in to testify I bought a box of copper jackets?"

"No, you didn't tell me that," Shigata said, thinking of at least three conversations in which that could have been mentioned. "Was it true?"

"Oh, yeah, it was true," Hansen said. "It was months before any of this happened. Shipp handed me a twenty and told me to go across the street and get him a box of cartridges."

"So you did," one of the younger FBI agents said. "And it just happened to be copper jackets."

"When you're a sergeant and the chief tells you to go across the street and buy him some cartridges, you do," Hansen said. "And I got him copper jackets because that's what he uses, of course. That doesn't mean he's the one who killed my wife. I just can't figure out who the hell—"

"Dan Buchanan?" Quinn offered, his voice uncertain.

Hansen shook his head. "Buchanan wouldn't have any reason. Anyway, why would he mind throwing Buchanan to the wolves now? Buchanan's dead. . . . Fugue state?"

"What's a fugue state?" Quinn asked.

"It's a psychological term," Shigata said. "A person in a fugue state can do something and hardly even know then he's doing it, much less remember it later. Is that what you think, Hansen?"

Hansen shook his head. "But don't ask me what I think. I damn well don't know. Shipp knows. I'm sure of that. But I don't know. Once we get the lab report on those slugs—It's got to be his gun. It's got to be—"

"Why would it be his gun if he didn't do it?" Quinn inquired.

"Damned if I know," Hansen said. "I just can't think of anything else that would flip him out like that."

Quinn chuckled, a surprising sound in the grimness. "Unless he was driving around with evidence of some other crime and wanted to make sure nobody got a good look at his truck. We had any hit-and-runs lately?"

"No," Shigata said. "Neither has anybody else in the

county. That's a little farfetched."

"So's the rest of this mess," Hansen said.

Barlow shook his head and reached for the telephone.

"Do you need anything else?" Shigata asked him.

"Yeah," Barlow said. "The privacy to make some telephone calls without being overheard."

"You've got it," Shigata said. "The rest of us will move back to the squad room."

"Wait a minute," Barlow said. "We've still got to know for sure on that woman, what was her name, Shelley Morgan. Did you kill her, Hansen?"

"No," Hansen said, and then grinned. "But, of course, I'd say that if I did."

"Do you have any reasons yet on her?" Barlow asked. "Reasons why anybody'd want to kill her, I mean?"

"Well," Hansen said, "if I'd done it, I guess it would be because she lied at my trial. Since I didn't, my guess is Shipp. But I don't know why he would want to."

"Todd," Shigata said, "do you know who any of your aunt's clients were?"

"Uh-uh," Todd said. "She told me that was none of my business."

"That's what we needed the search warrant for," Shigata told Barlow. "If it was business-related, the answer'll be in her office."

Barlow looked at his watch. "What time did that Ranger leave for Austin? Would he have had time to get there yet?"

"Maybe," Quinn said.

Barlow, sitting in Shigata's chair, hit the speakerphone switch and started dialing again.

"Department of Public Safety," said the tinny voice on the other end.

"Ballistics," Barlow said.

"I'm sorry?"

"Let me speak to the ballistics person. The firearms examiner."

"Hold one moment. . . . That line is busy. Would you like to hold?"

150

"I would like you to cut in."

"I'm sorry, sir, I am not allowed to do that. Would you care to hold?"

It took another ten minutes to find out that the copper-jacketed slug that killed Shelley Morgan was from the same gun—definitely a Smith & Wesson, further details not yet determined—that fired the copper-jacketed slugs that killed Lillian Hansen, Gaylene Hansen/Shipp, and a cocker spaniel named Honey, and that they positively were not fired from either of the submitted firearms, which demonstrably were not Smith & Wessons.

"*Now* I want the room to myself," Barlow said.

He took half an hour behind closed doors, while everybody else waited and fidgeted. During that time he made a number of outgoing calls; twice, the telephone rang. The first time he talked a long time, too quietly to be overheard outside the office, but the second time he shouted, "What?" Then he stepped to the door and said, "Mark, you better hear this."

Shigata went to the telephone. In a few minutes he came back out to the squad room. "The slugs Quinn collected in the street were not fired from the same pistol as the fatal slugs," he said. "They were fired from a Smith and Wesson too, but a different one. We're back to square one."

Hansen stared at him, his face looking suddenly ten years older.

"What does that mean?" Todd asked. "How could—"

"It means Shipp could have another pistol," Hansen said, "or I could have another pistol."

"But if the firearms residue test was negative, like that lady said—"

"With the old paraffin test," Hansen answered, "we got a lot of false positives. You could get a false positive if you'd been working with fertilizer or changing a baby's diaper. With the new tests, you get a lot of false negatives. You don't if you run a real neutron-activation analysis, but I don't guess they did."

"Why wouldn't they?" Todd demanded.

"Because they're too expensive to use every day. They're

too expensive." Hansen's voice broke, and he covered his eyes with the thumb and forefinger of his right hand.

"Steve, we're not through," Quinn said. "We're not through yet by a long shot."

"I know," Hansen said. He lowered his hand to the table top, clenched and unclenched his fist. "I'm okay. What do you want me to do while you go serve those search warrants? If it'd make the paperwork easier for me to sit in a cell, I don't mind."

"The hell you don't mind," Quinn said. "You don't mind just like I wouldn't mind going back to a bamboo cage in Vietnam."

"You do what you have to do," Hansen said, his voice still uneven. "You can stand whatever you have to stand. You endure or die. And the world doesn't give a shit which one it is. There's seven billion people on this earth. One more or less doesn't make that much difference. Send not to ask for whom the bell tolls, it doesn't toll for anybody anymore. Okay, okay, okay, I'm all right, I was just— stunned, that's all. I had started to believe this nightmare was about over."

"It is," Barlow said. "Look, we've got steps we go through, okay? To start with, I'm not even supposed to be on this myself. I'm supposed to have assigned an agent to it. We're supposed to reinterview all the witnesses, if we're going for a civil-rights case. But who's to interview? I've talked to you. I've talked to Todd. I've talked to Donna Gentry. I've talked to that firearms examiner in Austin. I can't talk to, what's his name, Dan Buchanan, because he's dead. I can't talk to Shipp because he's on the run, having, shall we say, behaved indiscreetly this morning in front of a police chief and a Texas Ranger. I've talked to everybody involved. I've got reports on everything I can get reports on, and then some. You've all told me there is substantial evidence that Hansen's civil rights have been violated, and obviously you're right. Now, as I see it, we have three things going on at once, and only one of them is *really* mine. We've got a civil-rights case I frankly don't see a hill of beans of sense in working, because nobody involved in the violation is now in any position of authority."

Shigata opened his mouth to speak, and Barlow said, "Wait a minute. Let me finish what I'm saying. We've got a tax case—Shipp spending a lot more than he was making—but that at best is going to take months to work. I intend to serve those search warrants and you're welcome to go along with me, but it's not going to get you anywhere fast. And we've got the goal of getting Hansen out of jail legally. Now, what's top priority, in terms of scheduling?"

"Getting Shipp," Hansen said.

"Getting Hansen off the hook," Shigata said. "We can get Shipp later. But that was what I wanted the civil-rights investigation for, to get—"

"Mark," Barlow said in a rather reproachful voice. "And you an attorney. Think."

Shigata reached across the table and picked up the file, which at the moment was in front of Quinn. He went into his office and shut his door.

"What's he doing?" Todd asked.

Barlow, looking rather pleased, said, "Thinking." He stood up. "Todd, does—did your aunt have a computer?"

"Yes, sir. It's an IBM."

"Good. Quinn, you can come with us if you want to. We're going over to Morgan's Accounting Services."

"Hadn't I better tell the chief—"

"You're not on duty," Hansen interrupted. "Anyway, I'll tell him."

"Yeah, but—"

"Suit yourself," Barlow said. "We're going to serve that first warrant. Todd, do you have a key?"

"No, sir."

"Quinn, were there keys in her purse?"

"We didn't find her purse," Quinn said. "It wasn't in the car or with the body."

"Uh-oh," Barlow said. "And she was hit sometime yesterday—"

* * *

153

Shigata came out of the office with a dark-brown leather folder under his arm and several small items in his hand. "Where'd everybody go?" he asked.

"Over to Shelley's office," Hansen said.

"Quinn too?"

"Yes."

"Okay," Shigata said, "we're going over to Galveston. I want you to take charge of some things for me."

"Okay," Hansen said, "what?"

"These," Shigata said. "They were in my lap drawer. They came with the desk." He handed over Hansen's driver's license (unexpired), his police identification card, and his badge. "I think you'll be able to keep them. What did you do, renew the driver's license a week before all this happened?"

"Not even a week," Hansen said. "Two days. What are we going to Galveston for?"

"Well," Shigata said, "I called the D.A.'s office. I had quite a few things to say. I told them I might—*might*—be able to talk you out of suing the county if they could get this cleared up fast. So the D.A.'s office called a judge or two or three, and miraculously a spot opened up on the docket. See, the thing is, a motion to set aside a conviction usually comes from the defense attorney and the courts usually don't pay a whole lot of attention to it, unless some pretty strong evidence is presented. But when the motion comes from the *prosecution*—you see what I mean?"

"Shigata, how are you pulling this? I mean, with that firearms evidence we got today—"

"Vacating a verdict doesn't change the verdict," Shigata said. "It just, in effect, declares that the results of that particular trial are now deemed to be invalid. Retrying you would not constitute double jeopardy. But in the meantime, you walk." He unlocked the passenger's door of the Bronco and watched Hansen and Todd climb in.

"So what about the other stuff?" Hansen asked out the window.

Shigata waited until he was in the car, too, before asking, "What other stuff?"

154

"Escape. Taking Claiborne's property, even if I did return it. Breaking into city hall. I guess that's all, unless they want to charge me for getting rid of a prison shirt and jacket. They can have the pants back."

"Do you really think anybody's going to bother about any of that?" Shigata asked. "I don't think you fully realize your legal position right now."

"I guess I don't."

"You've got grounds for a whopping-big lawsuit against the city of Bayport, Galveston County, and the State of Texas."

"You know as well as I do nobody can sue a governmental agency unless that agency consents to be sued."

"There's this other big court called public opinion. You could do a lot of damage there too."

"Shigata, I don't want any of that. All I want is to get on with my life."

"That doesn't mean I can't use it as a weapon."

There was no sign left of the Friday-night storm that had closed the causeway. The sky was brilliantly clear, and the water far below was blindingly bright. In Galveston, the palm trees, always made unhappy by freezing temperatures, were drooping their fronds, but most of the roadside growth had weathered the storm. The usual cluster of birds sat on the statues in the middle of the street. But Hansen wasn't enjoying the serenity of the scene. As they parked beside the court building, he was afraid he was going to vomit from sheer nerves.

"Well, that's that," Barlow said in a thoroughly disgusted voice. "Any luck, Jeff?"

FBI agent Jeff Thompson looked up, his face blackened by fingerprint powder, and said, "Gloves."

"Predictable."

Shelley Morgan's computer was gone. So were all her computer disks. So were all—literally all—of her files. Empty filing-cabinet drawers gaped open.

"I'm sorry we didn't get to it sooner," Quinn said, "but

155

with everything else going on—"

"It probably wouldn't have done any good," Barlow said. "If you didn't get the report she was missing until after midnight and she'd been missing twelve hours by then, it was probably gone before you knew she was gone."

"Most likely," Quinn said. "But that doesn't make me any happier."

"Does Hansen have any gloves?" Barlow asked, elaborately casually.

"I suppose he does," Quinn said, equally casually, "at home. But the place hasn't been opened in three and a half years, and with the storm we had last fall, well, I would kind of doubt they'd be wearable."

"You know what I mean," Barlow said.

"I haven't seen him in gloves," Quinn said. "And I do know where his stash was. If you want to go look."

"Legal?" Barlow asked.

Quinn shrugged. "How should I know? It's in a place under my control, and not legally under his control. At least not right now. So I guess it's legal."

"Then lead me to it."

"I'm sorry," Hansen said. "It's just nerves."

"It's okay," Shigata answered. He was standing in the open door to a restroom stall, attempting with no great success to avoid watching Hansen vomit.

"Keep Todd out of here," Hansen said, and then retched again.

"I sent him to get you a Coke. I figure it'll take him a little time to find the machines."

"Oh, *shit*," Hansen said. "You'd think I'd stop this after a while. I'm just so scared. I'm so bloody *scared*. I wasn't this scared during the trial, so why—*shit*, here I go again— Keep Todd out of here—sorry I'm such a coward—"

"You're not a coward," Shigata said. He ran water over a wad of paper towels. "Here, wash your face. If you think you're bad, you should have seen me when I realized they thought I'd killed Wendy. I went into shock so bad they

156

thought I was having a heart attack, and they gave me a shot to knock me out and then put me in the hospital overnight."

"Yeah?" Hansen said, looking up with some interest.

A bailiff stuck his head into the rest room. "Is he still puking?"

"I think he's about through," Shigata said.

"Okay," the bailiff said, and shut the door.

"You know," Hansen said, getting to his feet, "that's what I keep coming back to—what puzzles me the most about this whole thing."

"You lost me," Shigata said.

Hansen cupped his hands under the water faucet, rinsed his mouth, and then said, "Shipp. He was as bad in shock as I was that morning. And he hated me. I'm not kidding. He hated me right then as bad as I've ever seen one man hate another."

"But we know he was there during the night," Shigata said. "Todd saw him leaving."

"Did he?" Hansen asked, standing straight. "Sure, there was some moonlight that night, and a person can see a little by that and starlight, but how much? Really? Did he really see Shipp? Or did he just see Shipp's truck—or car? Or maybe even just a truck or car that looked like Shipp's? I am sure Gaylene was pregnant by Shipp, but that doesn't prove he was there."

"You were reading 'The Cenci' during the trial," Shigata interrupted as Todd came in with a Coke.

"How'd you know that?"

"Quinn told me. And then I didn't know Gaylene was your stepdaughter. I thought she was your daughter. So you can guess what I was thinking."

"Quinn never read 'The Cenci,' " Hansen said.

"What's it about?" Todd asked. "And why did that make Mr. Shigata think—"

"It's a verse play based on a real case. It's about a girl who arranged to have her father murdered because her father had been raping her," Hansen said. "Hey, Shigata, do you know what the son of a bitch who edited Benet's *Reader's Ency-*

clopedia said about that?"

"I don't even know what Benet's *Reader's Encyclopedia* is," Shigata replied, "but I suppose you're going to tell me anyway."

"He said Beatrice Cenci's attorney had 'falsely claimed that Francesco had tried to commit incest with her.' That really pissed me. I mean, with him a Roman nobleman and her just twenty-one with nobody on her side but her stepmother who was even more scared that she was—I've read up on the case. While I was in prison, I mean. Like how much evidence do you expect to find four hundred years later? She was twenty-one. Girls got married then at fourteen. How come Francesco didn't try to find a husband for her? How come he kept her locked up—"

"Hansen," Shigata interrupted, " can we work one case at a time? Let's get you out of prison and Shipp in before we attempt to retry Beatrice Cenci."

"She was executed, you know."

"Four hundred years ago," Shigata said. "I don't think we can do much about it now."

"Maybe I'll write a book about it."

"Fine," Shigata said, beginning to have some idea why Hansen had never made it past sergeant. "But do it on your own time. Do you think we can make it into the courtroom now?"

"Yeah." Hansen grinned a trifle shamefacedly. "Sometimes I forget I'm not supposed to be a scholar anymore."

"You're welcome to clear Beatrice Cenci," Shigata said, "as long as you do it on your own time. But let me know before you start on Lizzie Borden."

"She was acquitted." Hansen said vaguely. "But I think she was guilty all the same." He sat down on the wooden bench seat beside Shigata. Todd was on the other side of him; Assistant District Attorney Diego Escobar, new since Hansen had policed in Galveston County, was on the other side of Shigata.

"All rise," the bailiff intoned, and before anybody had a chance to stand Judge Walter Andrews had whisked in and seated himself, to inform everyone, in a rather bored tone, that court was now in session.

"I understand what we have here is a petition to set aside two verdicts of guilty in two cases of capital murder. Who is representing the defendant?"

Shigata rose. "I am, your honor."

The judge looked at him. "Mr. Shigata. I was under the impression you were the police chief in Bayport."

"I am, your honor."

"It was the former Bayport police chief who—"

"Yes, sir," Shigata interrupted. "And we now have evidence to show that a gross miscarriage of justice occurred. If necessary, we can call witnesses; however, all the documentary evidence is here."

"What does the prosecution say?"

Escobar rose. "Your honor, this is a prosecution motion."

"A *prosecution*—" The judge, sounding genuinely surprised, rapidly leafed through papers. "So it is. Well. That, of course, puts a different light on things. So the *prosecution* would like the verdict vacated?"

"Yes, your honor. We are convinced there was a serious miscarriage of justice. Very important evidence was concealed."

"So you are saying the defendant is innocent?"

Escobar hesitated. "We are saying there definitely was not sufficient evidence to prosecute, and considerable evidence tending in the other direction was concealed. We would like to leave the door open to retry the case later if such should prove necessary. But at this time we request that the verdict be vacated and the defendant be discharged."

"There are no motions to the contrary from anyone?" Judge Andrews inquired, looking around the courtroom. "In that case the petition is granted. If the clerk of the court will prepare—"

It was over. That fast. It hadn't taken five minutes; the press had not even had time to gather. One lone reporter who had been hanging around the courtroom for something else entirely raced for a telephone, as Shigata and Hansen

159

followed into the judge's office to wait for signatures. "Dad?" Todd answered. "Does that mean you don't have to go back to Huntsville or anything like that?"

"That's what it means," Hansen said. He sat, rather abruptly, in a chair in Judge Andrew's private office. "Shigata, I can't stop shaking. I don't know why, but I can't stop shaking. What am I doing trying to get shocky now?"

"We'll get you some coffee after we get out of here," Shigata said.

"Yeah," Hansen said, and leaned over with his head on his knees. That was the recommended position for somebody about to faint, but Shigata wasn't sure how much good it would do for somebody about to go into shock. His last first-aid class had been a long time ago.

The judge's secretary—also new since the last time Hansen had been in this office—came in, bringing coffee and sympathy, and Hansen sat up to drink the coffee. He stopped shaking moments before the judge came out, to hand over a signed legal paper. "The original is being filed right now," he said. "And I must say I'm delighted with this turn of events, Sergeant." He looked at Shigata. "It is sergeant again?"

"Oh, yes," Shigata said.

"Thank you," Hansen said, still sounding a little bewildered.

The wait allowed three reporters time to gather, and Hansen obligingly paused on the front steps long enough to say that he was delighted and had work to do. In the car, he asked, "What did they expect me to say?"

"They knew what you'd say," Shigata answered, backing the car. "They just wanted a picture of you saying it. I want to swing by the docks long enough to see if Hoa's in port."

"I don't want—" Todd began.

"What you want isn't the question," Hansen said. "I don't want you anywhere Shipp can find you until we find Shipp."

But Shigata paused at a shrimp-boat slip, said "Damn!" and turned the car around. "Car one's ten-eight en route back to the city," he told the radio.

160

Quinn answered instantly. "Car two to car one. What happened?"

"Mission accomplished. Call the payroll clerk and tell her to pull the old records and reinstate him effective today. What's going on there?"

"We served the first search warrant. It was a wipe. Literally everything was gone. We're waiting on the second until you get back to go along."

"Any news on Shipp?"

"Nothing. We put him on NCIC. I went on and wrote up a warrant charging him with assault."

"On what basis? Because then he was technically legal trying to stop Hansen."

"I know that. On the basis that Phillips was in the patrol car when he rammed it."

"Okay. Find Hansen a pistol; both of his are in Austin."

"Ten-four," said Quinn enthusiastically. "I've got two up here; he can use one of mine."

"Ten-four." Shigata hung the microphone back in its holder, glanced at Hansen, and said, "What about Constance Kent?"

"Who? Oh, yeah. That case in England. Eighteen—I forget eighteen what. Did you know Dickens and Wilkie Collins both based fictional detectives on the Scotland Yarder in that case?"

"I just wondered if you were going to rework that one too."

"Oh. Uh-uh. At least not until I rework Beatrice Cenci."

"And Lizzie Borden?"

"It's been reworked enough. Shigata, you mind if we rework mine before I rework the Cencis?"

"That sounds to me like a real good idea," Shigata said. "You were serious when you said you still weren't convinced Shipp did it?"

"Yes." Hansen glanced in the back seat. "Todd, you remember that night, when you were coming back from wherever it was you and Ted Zimmer sneaked off to, you said you saw Shipp leaving?"

"Yeah."

161

"Did you see Shipp himself, or just his truck?"

"It wasn't his truck. It was his car. No, it was too dark to see him. Just the car. But I know it was his because you know those personalized license plates he used to have, I saw them and I know it was him."

"Personalized license plates?" Shigata asked.

"Yes," Hansen said, "they were pretty unforgettable. On the truck he had DALSHIP and on the car he had CELSHIP. And it was the car you saw, Todd? You sure? Positively not the truck?"

"I'm sure," Todd said." It was the car."

"I need to do some thinking about that," Shigata said. He stopped in front of the motel. "You're out of uniform, Sergeant. Take care of that right quick."

Chapter 11

"I DON'T WANT TO serve this search warrant now," Barlow announced.

"Okay," Shigata said.

"I'm not working your case. Serving the search warrant now might help you, but it would blow my case—if I even have a case—right out of the water. My people need to spend at least two months checking other things before we're even ready to think about—"

"Okay," Shigata said.

"You wanted Hansen out of jail. You've got Hansen out of jail. You didn't need me for that to start with, if you'd taken two minutes to think."

"Okay," Shigata said for the third time. "The problem was we didn't *have* two minutes to think. We aren't like you. You've got just about all the manpower you could need, and the financial base of the federal government, weakened reed through it is. That makes things different. Look at Bayport. Look at what we've got. We've got one more experienced officer than we had yesterday. That's going to help. But I don't know how much."

"So you don't mind if we pack up and go home," Barlow said.

"It wouldn't do me much good if I did mind. But no, I don't mind."

"I'm going home," Melissa said. "Mark, he might hide out for three months. You can't expect me to stay here that long."

"I suppose you're right," Shigata said. "But keep that pistol near you, just in case."

"He doesn't want me. You were only afraid to start with that he might come after you because of the evidence. But if he has a radio or a television or a newspaper he knows it's too late for that now. And he won't indulge in gratuitous killings. Everything he does has a purpose. You know that, if you know anything at all about him."

Shigata did know that. But it didn't make him any happier as he hung up the telephone and resumed thinking.

What to do. What to do. What to do.

When he was in the FBI, there were huge books full of rules to follow. Or he asked the SAC if he didn't know what to do and the books didn't tell him. And if the SAC wasn't sure either the question was bounced upstairs, to the research division or the legal division. Or, if necessary, to the Attorney General of the United States. Or even, if necessary, to the President.

Here, theoretically, he could ask the mayor, but she would tell him to use his own judgment. She was a former third-grade teacher. She didn't know anything about law enforcement. Theoretically he could ask the city attorney, but he was a part-timer who spent most of his time dealing with the civil law. He didn't know much about criminal law, anything about enforcing it.

So in reality Shigata was where the buck stopped. Most of the time he enjoyed that. But there's a limit to how much, or how well, a man could think when he was half dead on his feet from lack of sleep, and it felt like he and Quinn both had been in that condition for the last six months. On top of that, he didn't know how he was supposed to work a case while baby-sitting a sixteen-year-old, with everybody else apparently waiting for him to wave a magic wand and make everything all right.

He didn't have any magic wands to wave.

He wanted a look at the inside of Dale Shipp's house.

He wanted a look—again—at the inside of K and S Sporting Goods, which was a firm he would rejoice to see out of business.

He wanted Dale Shipp inside a cell, at least long enough for everybody else to have time to breathe, even if it was on a charge that wouldn't stick.

He couldn't figure out how he was going to get any of those things.

To get a search warrant, you need what the legalities refer to as "probable cause." He didn't have probable cause to get a search warrant for either Shipp's house or Shipp's gun-shop. He was riding on hunches. And while it might be true that the hunch of an experienced law-enforcement officer was probably more accurate than many a legal "probable cause," the fact remained that it held no legal validity. His own gut instinct right now was to tell everybody to go home and get a good night's sleep and try to think about this later.

He did have a valid *arrest* warrant for Dale Shipp, thanks to Quinn's decision that Shipp's act of ramming a police car containing a police officer constituted assault on the officer inside the car. But how far can you push an arrest warrant? It authorizes you to make an arrest. It does not, under normal situations, authorize you to go inside a house and look for somebody who might or might not be there. And it certainly does not authorize you to look for any *thing* that might or might not be there.

What he needed was three aspirins and a good night of sleep. A night not spent sitting up on the hall floor worrying.

He stepped to the door and looked out into the squad-room. Quinn and Hansen had their heads together over a map. Probably trying to figure out where Shipp could go to hide a yellow crew-cab pickup truck. "Todd, why didn't you go to school today?" he asked abruptly.

Todd caught the beanbag he had been kicking. "School let out at three-thirty," he said.

"That wasn't the question."

"I didn't want to."

Hansen looked up from the map. "Tomorrow you will want to."

"Where are we going to live?"

"What difference does that make to whether you go to school?"

"What school district?"

"You may safely assume you will remain in the Bayport ISD."

"We could live at Shelley's house. She doesn't need it anymore."

"You're a cold-blooded twerp, aren't you?" Quinn commented.

"Well, she doesn't."

"We are not going to live at Shelley's house. Todd, for a few days we'll live at a motel. But I'll be figuring out something."

"Anyway, I need to get my clothes. And my schoolbooks. And you didn't give me time to get my key to get back in with."

"You had plenty of time to get your key. You just chose to spend it arguing instead. Okay. Okay. We'll go get your clothes and schoolbooks."

"How, if I don't have my key?"

"Easily. That is, if I can get a car."

"Take fourteen," Shigata said. "Barndt usually drives it, but she doesn't come on till midnight."

After Hansen departed, Shigata sat down in the squad room across from Quinn. "Thank God for peace and quiet," he said.

"That kid's a handful, isn't he? Quinn agreed. "If he was mine, I'd have him out digging a garden. Looks to me like that aunt of his didn't get a lick of work out of him for three and a half years. Hansen's going to have fun knocking some sense back into him."

"Sixteen's a little late to start," Shigata said. " 'Didn't want' to go to school. I can't tell you what my dad would have done if I'd pulled that, because I never would have thought of it to start with."

"Oh, I pulled it," Quinn said. "Until I figured out if I was at home I got to walk behind the mule and if I was at school Daddy got to walk behind the mule."

"Walk behind the mule?"

"We had a mule-drawn plow," Quinn explained. "We plowed our garden and just about everybody else's around here. Nobody uses mule-drawn plows anymore. Garden tractors are cheaper. And you don't have to cope with the mule. I'd like to see Todd Hansen coping with a mule. There's this story my dad used to tell. A city fellow bought a mule and then he couldn't make it work. So he asked the country fellow he bought it from how to make it work. And the country fellow said, 'Well, first you've got to get the mule's attention. There are two or three ways of doing that. You might hit him in the head with a baseball bat. Or you might try building a fire under him.' See, that's Hansen's problem. First he's got to get Todd's attention."

"Fourteen to car one." Hansen's voice was shaking a little.

"Somebody got the mule's attention," Quinn said, as Shigata picked up the hand radio that was rarely very far from him.

"One, go ahead."

"Um—what we were looking for is where I was heading."

"Ten-four. Back off and wait. We're en route. All units, ten-three your traffic."

"Chief, you need backups?" Susa Gonzales, alert as ever.

"Negative right now, but stand by. On second thought, yes. Set up a roadblock at the I-45 on-ramp. Headquarters, get a county unit to back her up."

"Ten-four."

By that time Shigata and Quinn were in the Bronco. Shigata was driving; Quinn's wrist, incompletely recovered from a compound fracture in August, made high-speed driving a little difficult and a lot risky. "Chief, we need a backup in the alley," Quinn said.

"You're it. I don't want to put the address on the air. You know damn well he's got a scanner. I don't want to spook him."

"He's probably spooked already. Who else would we be looking for?"

"You have a point."

He had a point. Hansen shouted, "He's going east on Crockett, just turned north onto Fannin—" Hansen's siren was audible on the radio.

Shigata cut his siren on. "Stay on him. We're paralleling you on Bowie. Phillips, ten-twenty?"

"West on Zavala heading for the Fannin intersection. What am I looking for?"

"Yellow crew-cab pickup, one white male driver. Consider armed and very dangerous."

"Same one that rammed me this morning?"

"Affirmative."

"Ten-four." There was a certain satisfaction in Phillip's voice. One more person who would like to get a shot at Dale Shipp.

But Phillips was tired. He was doubling over, working two shifts in one day because the department was so short-handed. Even at his age—and he was young—his reflexes weren't going to be as good as normal.

Neither were Quinn's, or Shigata's, or Hansen's. And they weren't young.

On the other hand, Dale Shipp wasn't young either. But he was desperate.

Why was he so desperate?

If he had killed anybody, he'd used a different pistol than the one they'd tested to do it with. Suppose he *had* assaulted Gaylene. There was now no way, ever, to bring the crime home to him. The ground is wet in Galveston County. Even with embalming and a good casket, a body decays fast. There would be now no way to prove that Gaylene had ever had sex, no way to prove that she was in the very early stages of pregnancy. And even if those things could be proven, every

168

person who could have tied Shipp to the case was dead.

So why was he so desperate?

Who would he be trying to protect, if not himself?

Before he knew he had reached a decision, Shigata heard himself speaking into the radio. "All units, break off the chase."

"*What!*" Hansen's voice sounded unbelieving.

"You heard me, break off the chase. All units, twenty-nine at 1401 North Houston." Shipp's house.

"Chief, you know he heard that," Quinn said.

"I meant him to. Dale Shipp didn't kill those women. Celeste Shipp did."

"Are you crazy?"

"No. I'm sure. It fits. Who did—who *would*—Lillian call? Especially if she was as embarrassed and upset as Hansen said she was. Not her sister. Her sister couldn't do anything. Not Shipp. There was no chance at all of getting help from him. He'd *caused* the problem. He wasn't going to help solve it. Who would she call? Another woman. Somebody who would see herself as harmed as much as Lillian and Gaylene. Somebody who might be able to talk Shipp into helping, or might even be willing to provide the help herself. The *one* person in the world Lillian would think of who might be able to help. Whose car was it Todd saw leaving that night? Not Dale Shipp's. Celeste's. Of course Shipp was in shock that morning. Of course Shipp hated Hansen that morning. He really *didn't* know who did it. He really *didn't* know anything had happened until he got the call. He really *did* think Hansen did it—then. And even Hansen says Shipp loved Gaylene, even if it was a twisted, distorted love. But remember what Hansen said about the trial? Every time he turned his head, there was Shipp grinning at him—I forget exactly what he said, something like a spiteful grin. That wasn't hatred anymore. It was love of mischief, and it was Shipp knowing if Hansen took the rap, Celeste got out from under it. Even Shelley—would she stop for a man needing a lift? Not from all we've heard about her she wouldn't."

"If she knew him—" Quinn said.

"No," Shigata said firmly, "Not even then. But just about any woman," Shigata continued, "would stop for a respectable middle-aged woman with car trouble. Especially a woman she knew."

"So he loved Gaylene but he protected the woman who killed her."

"Who did he love more?"

"Himself," Quinn said. "If you knew him, you'd know that."

"So if Celeste went down, who would she take with her? That explains how he's been acting. With his finances—we all know he was spending a hell of a lot more than he was making. And *now* he knew we were going to be looking at him. Looking hard. So think about it. Shelley's office looted, his truck at Shelley's house—Celeste may've—probably did—kill Shelley as well as Lillian and Gaylene. But I'll bet you money it was Shipp that took Shelley's files. He wanted them gone before any of us could think of looking for them, to protect himself even more than Celeste. Even if he arranged a quiet little suicide for Celeste after she took care of Shelley, he wouldn't know what letters she—Celeste, I mean—might have left where."

"So now his empire is crumbling anyway. If you're right, we're going into a firefight."

"I know it."

"I'll bet you're not wearing a bulletproof vest."

"I'll bet you're not either. Phillips?" He spoke into the radio. "Block the north end of the alley. Gonzales, break off your present location and block the south end of the alley."

"What if she's already gone?"

"If she is, she is. I'm betting she isn't . . . . She isn't," he said triumphantly about two minutes later. The Pontiac with the personalized license plate, CELSHIP, was sitting in front of the house.

"Now what?" Quinn asked.

"Now we sit here. This is called a war of nerves."

"Yeah, well, while you're having a war of nerves, move your feet so's I can get the shotgun."

Car fourteen stopped nose to nose with the Bronco, and Hansen got out. "Celeste," he said to Shigata. "I got it about two seconds after you gave the address. I should have got it three years ago."

"Where's Todd?"

"I dropped him off at a 7-Eleven with a game box in an alcove and gave him ten dollars. By the time he's blown it all, this should be over."

"So there really is a use for video games," Quinn said thoughtfully. "I always did wonder what they were for. Oh boy. Here it comes."

"Out of the car," Shigata said quickly.

When the yellow crew-cab stopped, all three police officers were facing it. Quinn had the shotgun at a rest position; neither Shigata nor Hansen had drawn his pistol. They were all waiting.

Shipp didn't get out of the truck.

Shigata and his officers didn't move.

Shipp didn't get out of the truck.

Shigata and his officers didn't move.

"So they got you off, Hansen," Shipp said from the truck.

"That's right. They got me off."

"Then you got what you wanted. You've got no more problems."

"No. I didn't get what I wanted."

"Then what do you want? You're free. You've got your job back. You've got your kid back. What more do you want?"

"I want what you can't give me. I want my wife back."

"She was shoddy goods, Hansen. Damaged."

"I don't blame her for what you did. Any more than I blame Gaylene for what you did."

"I didn't do anything to Gaylene."

"Right. And that's why you saw to it she was buried without an autopsy. Because you were afraid blood tests would have shown whose baby she was carrying."

"Who would have cared? She was just like her mother. Cheap."

"Say whatever you want to. But you know the truth. And

so do I. And so does God."

"You really believe in a God? After all you've seen?"

"You can jeer till hell freezes over and the facts won't change one iota. If I died this minute and you lived a millionaire's life for the next forty years, I wouldn't trade places with you. There is good and there is evil. There is God and there is Satan. You chose which side you wanted. Well, so did I. I loved my wife, Shipp."

"I didn't kill her."

"I know you didn't," Hansen said. "I know who did. And so do you."

"You can't prove anything."

"How much do you want to bet on that?" Hansen asked. "Get out of the truck, Shipp."

"Make me."

"I don't have to make you. I don't care if you ever get out of the truck or if you turn around and drive away. Celeste's inside the house."

"Is she?"

Quinn, shotgun in hand, whirled just as the first shots from the AK-47 raked across the yard. Somebody yelled; he wasn't sure who, as he fired reflexively and the woman fell, her gray hair spattered with blood that splashed from her chest. There would be no more bursts from the AK-47. As Quinn mechanically walked forward to pick up the AK-47, he heard the roar of the souped-up engine as the pickup took off.

By the time he turned with the shotgun in one hand and the AK-47 in the other, Hansen and Shigata were gone in the Plymouth sedan police car, leaving him to follow in the Bronco. Sitting in the front seat, microphone in hand, he said, "Phillips, break off in the alley and come around to the front to sit on the scene. Gonzales, hold your position—no, move farther into the alley. Block the rear entrance to the house. Headquarters, call Galveston County and have them send out a team from the medical examiner's office. Get us some backups from the county. I don't want any news-hounds here."

He got back out of the Bronco and stood on the sidewalk.

There was blood on it, a trail of spatters leading to where car fourteen had been parked. Somebody had been hit. He didn't know whether it was Hansen or Shigata. Whoever it was apparently was still mobile. That could be either one of them. There were both very tough men.

He was supposed to be tough too.

But right now he felt as old and as fragile as the sphinx. He'd never killed a woman or a child. He'd never wanted to. Even in Vietnam when a favorite ploy of the Vietcong was to send women or children out carrying bombs, or to employ women and children as snipers, he'd never killed them. He'd always found a way not to.

He could have found a way not to this time, if he'd had time to think. But there wasn't time to think. An AK-47 doesn't give you time to think.

Not for the first time, he cursed anybody who would insist on laws that allowed military weapons to get into civilian hands. He was as much against gun control as most police were; he wanted civilians to be able to have handguns, rifles, shotguns. He was sure in his own mind that the reason why the Romanians were able to get rid of Ceaucescu, and why the Panamanians were able to guard their own neighborhoods while American troops were hunting Digbats and Noriega, but the Chinese students had been mowed down in unarmed thousands, was that in Romania and Panama there were a lot of guns in civilian hands, and in China there weren't. The best defense Quinn knew of against dictatorship, other than education, was an armed population.

But civilians don't need AK-47s. Or armor-piercing bullets. The NRA was wrong, wrong, wrong about that.

"I didn't want to kill her," he said to Phillips.

"Of course you didn't." Phillips said. "You did what you had to do. She'd have killed all three of you if you hadn't stopped her."

"Stop her, yes. But I didn't have to kill her."

"Obviously you did," Phillips said.

"Yeah. Obviously I did." *Things are so easy when you're twenty-two and the world is all black and white. The older you get the more shades of gray you see.*

He went back to the Bronco. "Car two to car one."

"One, go ahead. I've been trying to raise you."

"I was securing the scene. Ten-twenty?"

"He's going down the beach. We're staying behind him."

"Hot pursuit?"

"That's affirmative."

"Good. Because you're out of the city."

"We noticed."

"Ten-four. En route."

"Is he okay?" Hansen asked. "He sounded funny."

"He will be. Okay, I mean. I'm still not sure you ought to be—"

"I'm okay," Hansen insisted. *I'm not okay. This is the stupidest thing I've ever done in my life. As long as I keep my hand exactly where it is, he's going to think I was hit only once, in the left forearm, and that one really isn't bad, except it hurts like bloody hell.*

It's this other one, the one he's going to know I've got when I get out of the car, that's bad. I'm going to be in the hospital awhile from this one.

This one doesn't hurt much yet. I don't know if I'll be able to take it when it starts to.

I worked a case once, this guy got in a fight in a bar and he got shot in the abdomen and he just thought somebody hit him there and he went about his business for four hours and then collapsed. When it happened, I thought this guy has got to be the stupidest person in creation, how in the world could anybody get shot in the abdomen and not know it? Well, now I know how. I feel like somebody hit me in the stomach. Just a dull ache and a little breathless. Only, there wasn't a fist anywhere near me, so I know that what hit me wasn't a fist.

I ought to tell Shigata. I ought to get to a hospital. But I can stick it out a little bit longer. A little bit of time won't make that much difference.

How big a fuel tank does Shipp have? How full is it?

174

How big a fuel tank do we have? How full is it?

Shipp, stop the truck, stop the damned truck, so we can stop too. The siren makes my head hurt.

The road forked, and Shipp veered off on the left fork. "That road dead-ends," Hansen said, surprised that his voice sounded almost normal.

"Then we've got him," Shigata said. He turned the car broadside to the road and opened the car door. "I'm taking the right side. That'll be his left when he comes back out. You take the left."

"Okay," Hansen said.

It was getting harder to move now. His head felt as if he was somehow about to float off into space. But he could last a little longer. If he could keep his back turned away from Shigata, so Shigata couldn't see the exit hole—

"Does this road have a name?" Shigata asked.

"Heron Crossing Road," Hansen said. "Quinn'll know. I'm surprised Shipp didn't."

"Car two, we're off on Heron Crossing Road," Shigata said. "We're setting up a roadblock."

"Ten-four," Quinn said. "About three minutes."

I still feel a hundred years old.

Nguyen wants me to join the church she goes to. I'm not going to join it and say I'll do things I won't do. They want me to stop drinking. Well, I can do that. They want me to stop drinking coffee. That'll be harder, but I can do it. They want me to promise to pay a tithe. I don't know if I can or not. I keep trying to figure it out and I can't see a way I can do it, not with my salary and my responsibilities. I don't want to promise to do something and then not do it.

But now? Now! With this kind of blood guilt on me? I know the Bible is mistranslated. I know we're commanded not to murder, not commanded not to kill. I know that. I know that. I know that what I did today wasn't murder. But I never wanted to kill a woman.

A woman older than I am. A woman with gray hair.

A woman with gray hair and an AK-47.

I don't know what else I could have done. I don't know

what else I could have done. I don't know what else I could have done.

And if I ever do figure out, it's too late to do it, because I already did what I did.

Heron Crossing Road. What the hell did Shipp think he was doing taking off on Heron Crossing Road? Everybody knows that dead-ends.

Shigata wouldn't know, of course. Hansen must have told him. But there's no way Shipp wouldn't know.

Quinn turned left onto Heron Crossing Road. He stopped right off the main highway, because if they had a roadblock set up with fourteen and Shipp managed to get past it, which wouldn't be too hard with that big crew-cab, they'd need a car to go after him in. Which meant Quinn had a responsibility to see to it the Bronco wasn't totaled out too.

Cradling the shotgun, because he might need it even if right now he never wanted to see it again, he walked into the woods and found Hansen lying on his belly, head up and pistol in both hands, braced against the trunk of a fallen tree, with bright blood bubbling out of the exit wound on his back. "What the hell do you think you're doing?" he demanded.

"Shut up," Hansen said, sounding a little weak and a little breathless but otherwise normal. "He's got to come back this way. There's no other way for him to go."

"How did you get Shigata to let you pull this?"

"He doesn't know. He thinks it was just my arm that was hit. I made sure of that."

"Then you're a jackass. What's your blood type?"

"O positive. Why?"

"You know why. You damn fool, there's times to continue a chase and times to break one off."

"And a time to be born and a time to die."

"Your boy needs you alive."

"I am alive."

"You're crazy, you know that, man?"

"So I have been told. Here he comes—"

Automatically, Quinn brought the shotgun up into firing position.

The yellow crew-cab hit the Plymouth broadside and kept going. Or tried to.

Tried to, but he was going too fast and the road curved just past the roadblock and he was going too fast and he didn't have a seat belt on, so when the crew-cab rolled with a horrible slowness that seemed to last forever before it came to rest upside down in a thunderous silence, Shipp was thrown free.

Thrown free, so that he hit a small cypress tree and all three observers could hear the crack as his neck broke. In the suddenly resumed silence, papers from Shelley Morgan's files drifted about, falling languidly one at a time onto the ground. Covering Shipp, covering all the answers that now they would never get.

"Chief," Quinn said.

"Yeah?"

"One of us has to get Hansen to the hospital fast. The damn fool didn't bother to tell you he was gutshot."

"What?" Shigata said sharply, turning.

"I would have told you eventually," Hansen said apologetically. "I just wanted to get Shipp first."

"So who takes Hansen to the hospital, and who stays here till more help can get back?" Quinn asked.

"Why does anybody have to stay here?" Hansen asked. "If you just left Shipp here—I mean, you eat, I eat, the buzzards must also be fed."

"Be glad you're not feeding them yourself," Shigata advised. He glanced at the body lying beside the cypress tree. "Al, I guess you're stuck with it. Is that okay with you?"

"Sure. It'll give me some time to think." He sat down on the ground and then looked up. "Hansen, the Bronco's parked on the road. Sure you can get that far?"

"I can get that far," Hansen said, approximately five seconds before his knees buckled. So it was Quinn who walked back to the Bronco and drove it as far into the woods as he could get it, and helped Shigata get Hansen into the back.

Epilogue

"It was faster than you deserved," Quinn said. "You were only in the hospital three weeks. After the stunt you pulled—I mean, talk about stupid—"

"Thanks for looking after Todd."

"Don't thank me. Thank Nguyen. I didn't do much."

"Where are we going?"

"You're going home."

"I hate to mention this, but I don't have a—" Hansen stopped. "Quinn, I can't—"

"The city paid it off," Quinn said. "Shigata talked them into it. He pointed out that legally you have a claim on three and a half years of back salary. Since you'd told him you didn't intend to ask for it, the least anybody could do was make sure you had a place to live when you got out of the hospital. Nguyen and Melissa—and all the kids we could get our hands on—cleaned it up."

"Was that when you found where Gaylene's bullets went?"

"Uh-uh," Quinn said. "No, Shigata and me went out and found them while you were still in surgery. I figure Celeste was standing in Gaylene's bedroom door and Gaylene was backed up against the back wall. The gun was heavy and pulling to the right. All three slugs were in the sheetrock of the hall."

"And that sheetrock already had so many holes in it, from the kids horsing around—"

178

"Right," Quinn said. "That sheetrock already had so many holes in it nobody thought to check for bullets. Not after Celeste put Lillian's fingerprints on the gun and dropped it at Lillian's feet. To do Celeste justice, I don't think she meant to frame you."

"But Shipp didn't mind working it that way," Hansen said, "after Celeste told him the truth."

"I figure that was when he told Celeste about the diary," Quinn agreed. "I figure she hadn't known about that. And, of course, that's what he couldn't let you find."

"So when did you find it?"

"Same time we found the bullet holes," Quinn said.

"So we finally know why," Hansen said. "He couldn't let me find it. You're right about that." Hansen chuckled dryly, unsteadily. "He must have sweated while I still owned that house, before the bank foreclosed. It's a wonder he didn't kill me too."

"Then somebody else might have looked," Quinn said. "I just wonder why he didn't burn the house."

"Didn't you read the diary?"

"Part of it. I read till I started puking. That was when I brought it to you."

"She wrote in it that she told him she didn't keep it at home. And she didn't."

"We found it there," Quinn objected.

"Yeah. In her schoolbag. And she'd left that in her locker at school. The school gave it back to me, and I never looked in it."

"Why?"

"Why would I? The school got all the textbooks out, and she didn't have any library books. If the situation had been different—if she'd been hit by a car or something—I'd probably have gone through her bookbag. But as it was—I was too busy trying to stay alive."

"You figure Gaylene was trying to blackmail him?" Quinn asked.

"I don't want to think," Hansen said. "I don't want to think at all right now, okay, Quinn?"

179

"Okay," Quinn said. "I don't know if you'll want to go on living here. Probably you won't. I wouldn't if I were you. But it's a roof until you can sell it and find another place. We replanted your garden. I told Todd he's got to pull weeds. You're not up to it yet. Quit crying. You can't walk in the door crying."

"The hell I can't," Hansen said. But then he did quit crying. "What is he doing here?"

"I don't know. I guess we better ask him."

Hansen got out of the car and walked over to Rusty Claiborne, who was leaning against the fender of a Huntsville State Prison station wagon. "Hi, Rusty," he said.

"I don't guess you much wanted to see me," Claiborne said, "but you left some books and stuff in Huntsville, and I didn't know if you were through reading 'em yet. So I brought them down for you."

"Thanks," Hansen said. "I wasn't quite through reading them."

"What's this here PMLA magazine?" Claiborne asked. "I looked in some, but I didn't see any pictures."

"It doesn't usually print pictures," Hansen said. "It's mainly for college professors and people like that."

"Oh," Claiborne said. "I thought it might be something like that. Man, you have the damnedest books I ever seen. Oh, by the way, thanks for the twenty. I kinda needed it."

"I thought maybe you would." *Now I want you to leave. I don't have anything against you. But you remind me too much of what I want to forget.*

Claiborne walked around to the front door of the station wagon, got in it, and drove away.

Quinn got in the police car and drove away.

It was ten o' clock in the morning. Todd was in school. At least, Todd better be in school.

Hansen had some time to himself.

And I damn sure need it.

Because things were not all right. Maybe, sometime in the future, things would begin to feel normal. But right now, Steven Hansen didn't know what normal was. What with